C. E. Morgan holds a master's in theological studies from Harvard Divinity School. She lives in Kentucky.

ALL THE LIVING

One summer, a young woman travels to the isolated tobacco farm her lover has inherited. As Orren works to save the farm from drought, Aloma struggles with loneliness and tries to find her way in a combative, erotically charged relationship with a grieving, taciturn man. Her growing sense of dissatisfaction is further complicated by her friendship with a dynamic young preacher. As she considers whether to stay with Orren or to leave, she grapples with the finality of loss and death, and the eternal question of whether it is better to fight for freedom or to submit to love.

C. E. MORGAN

ALL THE LIVING

Complete and Unabridged

ULVERSCROFT
Leicester

First published in Great Britain in 2009 by
Fourth Estate
An imprint of HarperCollins*Publishers*
London

First Large Print Edition
published 2010
by arrangement with
HarperCollins*Publishers*
London

British Library CIP Data

Morgan, C. E., *1976 –*
   All the living.
   1. Bereavement- -Fiction. 2. Man-women relationships- -
   Fiction. 3. Tobacco farms- -Kentucky- -Fiction.
   4. Large type books.
   I. Title
   813.6–dc22

   ISBN 978–1–44480–213–9

Published by
F. A. Thorpe (Publishing)
Anstey, Leicestershire
Set by Words & Graphics Ltd.
Anstey, Leicestershire
Printed and bound in Great Britain by
T. J. International Ltd., Padstow, Cornwall

This book is printed on acid-free paper

For P.

Special thanks to Adam Clay Griffey — CEM

This is an evil in all that happens under the sun, that the same fate comes to everyone. Moreover; the hearts of all are full of evil; madness is in their hearts while they live, and after that they go to the dead. But whoever is joined with all the living has hope, for a living dog is better than a dead lion.

— ECCLESIASTES 9:3

She had never lived in a house and now, seeing the thing, she was no longer sure she wanted to. It was the right house, she knew it was. It was as he had described. She shielded her eyes as she drove the long slope, her truck jolting and bucking as she approached. The bottomland yawned into view and she saw the fields where the young tobacco faltered on the drybeat earth, the ridge beyond. All around the soil had leached to chalky dust under the sun. She looked for the newer, smaller house that Orren had told her of, but she did not see it, only the old listing structure before her and the fields and the slope of tall grasses that fronted the house. She parked her truck and stared, her tongue troubled the inside of her teeth. The house cast no shadow in the bare noon light.

The ragged porch clung weakly to the wall of the building, its floorboards lining out from the door, their splintering gray now naked to the elements that first undressed them. When she tested a board with one foot, the wood ached and sounded under her, but did not move. She picked her way around a

1

mud-spattered posthole digger and a length of chicken wire to reach the door where she found a paper heart taped to the wood. The shape of the thing gave her pause. She read the note without touching it.

Aloma,
If you come when I'm gone, the tractor busted and I went to Hansonville for parts. Go on in. I will come back soon,
Orren

In this house, she thought, or the new one? She straightened up and hesitated. Over her head a porch fan hung spinless, trailing its cobwebs like old hair, its spiders gone. She turned to peer behind her down the gravel drive. Displaced dust still hung close behind the fender of her truck, loath to lie down in boredom again. It was quiet, both on the buckling blacktop road where not a single car had passed since she'd driven up, and here on the porch where the breezeless day was silent. A few midday insects spoke and that was all. She turned around and walked into the house.

If it was abandoned, it was not empty. Curtains hung bleached to gray and tattered rugs scattered across the floor. Against one wall, nestled under the rise of a staircase and a high landing, stood an old upright piano. One sulling eyebrow rose. Orren had told her of a piano on the property, one she could practice on, but it could not be this. Aloma edged past its sunken frame, leaving it untouched, and walked back through a dining room washed in south light past a table papered with bills and letters, into the kitchen. The ceiling here was high and white. It seemed clean mostly because it was empty — spacious and empty as a church. She circled the room, tugged open drawers and cabinets, but her eyes stared at their contents unseeing, her mind wheeling backward. She turned on her heel and stalked to the first room. She tossed back the fallboard and reached her fingers to the ivory. The keys stuttered to the bed, fractionally apart beneath her fingers, and it was no more, no less than she had expected. The sound was spoiled like a meat. She slapped the fallboard down, wood on wood clapped out into the echoing house in cracking waves, and then it was gone. She turned away with the air of someone halfheartedly resigned to endure, but as she turned, she started and stopped. A wall of faces stood before her, photographs in frames armied around a blackened mantel, eyes from floor to ceiling. She studied them without stepping closer. They gazed back.

She left the room as quick as she had come, retraced her steps to the kitchen where she had spied a door that led outside. She opened it wide to the June day. From where she stood, she claimed a long view of the back property. A field of tobacco began down a slope a hundred yards from the house and a fallow field neighbored close by, its beds risen like new graves. There a black curing barn stood and from its rafters a bit of tobacco hung like browned bird wings, pinions down, too early and out of season, she could not say why. To her left another barn, this one red, with a large gated pen and a gallery on one side. The pasture was empty. The cows had all wandered up a hillside to a stand of brazen green trees and stood blackly on the fringe of its shade gazing out, their bodies in the cloaking dark but their heads shined to a high gloss like black pennies in the sunlight. Far below their unmoving faces the newer house pointed south, no larger than a doublewide, no taller, no prettier. It banked the barbed edge of the cows' pasture. But none of this held Aloma's gaze for more than a moment. Instead, she looked out into the distance where, because she could not will them away or otherwise erase them from the earth, the spiny ridges of the mountains stood. She laughed a laugh without humor. All her hopes, and there they were. Had they been any closer, she'd have suffered to hear them laughing back.

★ ★ ★

When he came, she saw the sun flashes between the farthest trees where the road ran out of the north and she stepped forward and waited. Her eyes worried the spot where the tree-line ended. Then when the truck shot free from the last trees and she knew that it was his, she took another step forward and her hands came together of their own accord, but she did not leave the porch. His truck, as familiar to her as a face, turned in the drive, the glass glinted. Her eyes followed his progress up the hill, the dust rolling and sweeping low to the ground in blond curls behind his truck, then flanging and fading to nothing. At first she could see his figure only as a dark shape and the sun firing on the watch on his right arm as he turned the wheel. Then when he was finally before her, braking and leaning in slightly under the shade of the visor to pull the keys from the ignition, she found the broad contours of his face and the color of his skin, much browner than the last time she had seen him, the day after the funeral three weeks ago when he

5

came down to the school and sat beside her and set a question to her. He said, You'll come up? And she said, Yes, yes. And it don't matter if it's all out of order like it is? And she shook her head and took his blanched face in her hands and kissed him, and that had struck her later as an odd reversal, he usually being the one to reach out and pull her to him. But she'd thought of it only later when she recalled how his lips had not made any motion against hers. It aroused a feeling in her like fear, but so slight and quick to fade that she didn't recognize it for what it was. Now she could not take her eyes from him sitting motionless in the truck watching her as she watched him. She stepped off the porch, hesitant at first, but then half running until she was standing at his door, her hand on the burning chrome of the handle. The tips of his eyelashes were pale as straw now, bleached from the sun so it seemed he had no eyelashes at all, nothing to impede his gaze. She yanked open the door of the truck or he pushed it open and she was half sitting in his lap and they were kissing. She said his name. He said nothing against her mouth. When she pulled away, Aloma saw the hatchings around his eyes were deeper than before. He was drawn, even more so than after the funeral she had not attended because she had to accompany the school's choir to Grayson, the principal had not given her the day off, she had her commitments. They were not her people, after all.

Orren placed his hand on his own chest flat-palmed and she saw the dark line of dirt under his nails like earthen parentheses. He looked at her directly. He said, You been here long?

No, she said, I only just got here a half hour ago.

He gave her a little shove then so he could ease up out of the cab, and when he did, she saw there was something altered in his body. Sudden age had impressed itself on his frame. With something like embarrassment, she turned slightly to look elsewhere, but found her eyes unwilling to obey, wary of this new thing, and when he slammed the door and stood before her, they both appeared ill at ease for a moment as if sizing up their differences. Then Orren stepped in to close the space between them and kissed her again and she sought after his familiar tobaccoed breath. He took her hand and said, Come on. You seen the house?

Which one? she said, her hand pressed a slight resistance onto his.

The real one, he said and nodded up at the big house.

Yeah, she said slowly, thought to say something more, but desisted. She let him lead her around the side and she peeked at him as he looked up at the height of it, squinting, his thin lips flattening further. He hitched up the waistband of his jeans and he crossed his arms over his chest and she saw clearly she had been mistaken. He had not turned old in three weeks' time, it was as though someone had come along with a plane and sheered off all the extra that once cushioned him. He was like something corded, every movement curtailed. She had noticed this too that first day after the funeral when he stepped from his truck looking pared as a carving and just as stiff, though he'd felt the same under her hands when she held him. But there was something different in his carriage — he was newly fitted to his skeleton — something that she saw now was a lasting change and not just a momentary trick of grief. This new bounded self had banished the old.

At the rear of the house, Orren steered her down along the rutted path that led to the newer, smaller house. She stepped smart to match his pace, eager to see the inside and maybe show him how much she preferred it to the large and rambling structure behind them. But he stopped abruptly only partway down the path and she stumbled against him and put her hand on his hip to steady herself. Orren raised one arm and pointed out toward the hills.

It's us all the way to the ridge, right under, he said. From where they stood at the crown of the tobacco field, the whole of the back property spread before them. The tobacco, sallow and tawny too early on its undersides, ran halfway out to the ridge where it met the young corn with its young sprouts of hair that skirted the upslope. Between the rows, the dirt was pale as cocoa powder. A few cows had wandered down off the hillside and spread out still and easy in their late-afternoon pasture. They stood singly, one or two with their hides pressed to the fence, watching or perhaps not watching but gazing slackly beyond the strictures of the field. One stood half in and half out of the barn, undecided, unmoving.

Orren reached around and placed his forearm on the back of Aloma's neck. It was heavy and warm and she felt the imposing damp of his sweat.

This is ours now, he said. She swallowed and nodded, but then she said, That makes me a little scared.

No, don't be scared, he said and when she turned to face him, he suddenly looked so much older than she, though he was only three years her senior, that she felt her youth on her like a yoke.

＊　＊　＊

The store was only three miles from the house on the road to Hansonville, the town that straddled the county line twenty miles beyond. When she'd asked what was for dinner and Orren said eggs or peanut butter and not smiled for the irony of it, she took it upon herself to drive down the road in the thinning evening and find them something to eat. The store was a clapboard one-room with nothing else in sight but the trees and the fields and a few dogs that loped across the road farther up, road-raised and emaciated, just skin over legbone and brisket. Two aging pumps stood off to the side of the building. There were no other cars when Aloma parked. The only thing that moved was a sign that hung by a dog-tag chain in the window that read CHEAP TOBACCO, swinging on the false breeze of a fan. Inside, the store was split in two, one half a small grocery, the other a craft shop with rows of hand-painted gourds stenciled with Indian designs. They filled the store with the scent of autumn in summer.

Haddy, said the woman behind the counter. Aloma waved, head down and saying nothing, and steered a small buggy along the aisles. She found a ham in the cooler and some kind of green veined with bright red and a few more vegetables that she did not know the name of and had no idea how to cook. She picked up a dozen eggs and opened the carton to see if any of the shells were cracked, she had seen a cook at the school do that once. A white slab of fatback, a gallon of milk, half and half for herself because she was freed from that place, she could eat what she wanted, then a box of chocolate cereal as well. Behind the register, the woman and her hair watched in the bulging mirror tacked above a wall of potato chips. When Aloma's buggy was half full of things she didn't know how to prepare, she wheeled it to the counter.

Mind to put half this on the Fenton tab, she said, just as Orren had instructed her.

Oh, the woman said, taking another, closer look at her. Are you from up there, bless your heart.

Aloma nodded, regarded the woman.

Bless your heart, the woman said again. It's real sad about them. She said this with one hand to her high gray hair and the other upending a pencil over and over again.

That lady was real nice, she said. She

11

always set and talked awhile when she come in. And such pretty red hair. Sure had a lot of opinions, though. She watched Aloma as she said this, her lids ridden up so that Aloma could see too much of her eyeballs, big glossy things. Aloma only nodded again, slowly, clutching Orren's billfold in her hand.

It's terrible what people don't deserve.

Yes, said Aloma carefully. She didn't like to yesmam, it always tasted like something foul on her tongue.

The woman leaned over slightly, her lips pursing like a tight unblossomed flower the closer she came. Aloma did not lean back, she gripped the buggy tight.

Now, I don't mean to sound unchristian, but which one didn't die?

Aloma blinked a few times. Orren, she said.

Now, is he the little one?

Aloma looked at her in confusion. He's about yay high, she said, holding her hand a good four or five inches over her head.

The woman threw her head back and laughed. No, I'm saying, is he the old one or the little one?

Oh, Aloma said, the younger one.

You ain't from around here.

No, my people were from Cady Station.

The woman's eyebrows rose slowly to greet her hair. I sure can't hear that in your talk.

Well, I went to a school.

We all got schooling, darlin, the woman said coolly.

One of the mission schools, Aloma said, her eyes narrowing. They worked a few things out of us.

Uh-huh. And what else they learn you up at this school?

I learned to play piano.

Oh. The woman smiled again, the tight mouth easing. Now, that's a right useful thing for a girl to know.

Yes, said Aloma, pushing her buggy forward a little. It's a good thing for a girl to be useful. She did not smile. The woman straightened up and took her time inspecting this statement and then with no speed whatsoever used her pencil to punch the keys on the register to ring Aloma out. But her eyes stayed on Aloma as she did this, and when the question came, Aloma was waiting for it.

So that little one is your husband. It was a question switch-hitting as a statement.

Aloma did not blink this time. You're goddamn right he is, she said evenly and her face did not alter, but a flush ruddied her cheeks before she even finished her sentence. The woman's smile fell by increments until her lips were a little red slash across the

13

bottom half of her face. She uncurled one taloned hand, palm up. Sixteen ninety-five, she said. And instead of using the tab, Aloma paid her cash out of Orren's billfold, then picked up the bags, turned her back on the woman, and left without another word.

★　★　★

She was sent to the mission school the month before she turned a thankless twelve, not because her aunt and uncle couldn't handle her anymore, but because there were nine in the house now — the adults, their five children, one foster child, and Aloma. Her aunt and uncle had always been fine to her, they possessed a kind of hollow-headed decency that couldn't be disparaged. When they told her of the school, they were gentle as doctors, and their voices said, This won't hurt a bit, and in fact, it had not really, at least not that Aloma could recall. Only that first night she found that her eyes stung and to make them stop she turned facedown into her pillow and let them tear with her mouth open ragged against the cotton ticking, but in the morning her eyes were better and she did not cry again, at least not over that.

It was not that her aunt and uncle hadn't cared for her — they had never made her feel guilty for their taking her in when they had no money — but they'd cared in a middling, impersonal way that instinctively reserved their best for their own. During her first year at the school, they made their small familial efforts, they phoned her once a month on Sunday afternoons and sent little cartooned magazines from their church about crossing a wide river in a phalanx of other refugees or about Ruth and her numerous losses. Until she began to play piano, Aloma read these again and again, carefully, stacked them in neat piles under her steel-framed bed. She wondered what it meant to uncover a man's feet, to sleep in his bed, to travel to a far country, to see enemies drowned. She wondered what kind of luck was required to be someone other than the person you were born to be.

The school carried her into a deeper cleavage of the mountains than the one she had known at her uncle's trailer, which jagged out like an aluminum finger from a limestone wall topped by firs, bone out of bone. There the night carried on and on until ten in the morning, then the tip of the finger finally burned with its first sun. When she arrived at the school, Aloma shared a small concrete room with two other girls and here too the mountain walls staggered and threated up over them all. The sun did not appear in the wound of the holler until long past eleven where it remained until Spar Mountain, like a curtain of earth, cut the light before it could naturally sputter out. It was a chasmed world without the twin ceremonies of morning and evening.

Aloma lived in this dark place, a dark county in a dark state, and it pressed on her ceaselessly as a girl until she finally realized in a moment of prescience that someday adulthood would come with its great shuddering release and she would be free. Then she would leave and find a riseless place where nothing impeded the progress of the sun from the moment it rose in the east until it died out easily, dismissed into the west. That was what she wanted. That more than family, that more than friendship, that more than love. Just the kind of day that couldn't be recalled into premature darkness by the land.

The only thing she remembered fondly from her years at her uncle's trailer was a piano, old with a tiger-eye top, its weight causing the linoleum floor to sag. Her aunt played on Sundays after church and the children were made to sit, the restless grappling mass of them, and sing along. But the churchy songs soon bored Aloma, hymns were not enough, they contained the sound in a too-small box of predictable chords. She wanted to see her aunt's fingers spider up and down the length of the keyboard, from the woody lows to the tiny baby sounds of the upper register. She always wanted more than she was given and secretly wished her aunt's hands would slip and press two neighbor keys at once. It was always dissonance that she liked best.

When she learned that the settlement school offered a piano class, Aloma remembered the keys she had never heard struck — their tiny silent voices — and she was choked with desire for it. There were six pianos in the school and there would be six students in the beginning piano class. They let her in because she wrote PLEASE in big block letters at the bottom of her application and she pressed so hard with her fist that her pen tore through the paper and marked the laminate top of the desk.

In two years she had thoroughly impressed everyone, most of all herself. She had never been good at anything — not rotten, but not gifted either — so that she was eternally overlooked, and her new skill damped somewhat the sullen disposition her uncle had warned her teachers about. She had exhausted all the piano the school could offer

17

and she was sent twice a week to a woman in Perryville who had a piano degree from up East, but who had married a mine foreman and now played at a Baptist church and took students. The woman, Mrs. Boyle, had given her the Mozart and the Liszt that were now packed carefully away in the few boxes she had brought to the farm. She showed her how to arch her fingers so they fell in a swag from the platform of her hands and how to keep her shoulders down and loose and that yes, she was good, but that was only because she was in a backward place and she had much to learn if she ever wanted to get out and make music in what the woman called the real world. Yes, Aloma thought, that's where she was headed, to the real world. She felt a fierce want at the words. During the long unnatural nights, when the holler lay black under a sky lit far above the mountain walls, she thought about this, about other places. She tried to imagine exactly how leaving would feel. But it was so good, it promised such impossible pleasure, and all her pleasures so far had been such small lusterless things, that she found she could not imagine it all. The closest thing she could conjure was that it would be the exact opposite of lack, but even the hope of it did not feel the way she thought pleasure should, so she counted the nowhere days of her growing up and she waited.

Then after all her dreaming, when her final year arrived, she stared down her future with an unblinking eye. She had no money, no people to speak of. She wanted nothing more than to study the piano in some faraway place, but when the school asked her to continue after graduation and be the staff pianist for their music program, she agreed, because she had nowhere else to go and no way to get there. She ended up staying three years.

★ ★ ★

Before she knew Orren, she had waited for him. She stood in a line with the older teachers, impatient for the college farm boys to arrive, the assembly was waiting. But the boys were late. It was twenty-five miles as the crow flies, but they had not accounted for Slaughter Creek, its mad mountain-carved curves as it strove down from its headwaters to the larger Bondy River or its switchbacks that laxed the embankments and slapped against the road and the coal towns that hung precarious over its edges. The waters rose and flooded the gullible shantytowns each spring, flung trailers downstream and collected them there in tindered heaps like bleached and broken crayons. The creek churned and broke over rocks as it ran, it ran thick with forgotten things, appliances, hubcaps, dolls, animals, the debris of people who owned little worth remembering so the loss was barely noted. And along its rank spill, the coal trains escaped, black-topped, pollutive. Their hatched tracks crossed and recrossed the road that ate up three counties in its undulations, slowing the boys as they came, Orren at the wheel and driving hard against lost time.

When the boys crossed the last tracks and finally pulled into the school lot, they tumbled from the white van, yanking agricultural placards and pamphlets from the rear seats, and the teachers rushed forward to help them. Aloma followed, ostensibly to carry posters, but really to look at the boys and watch them move about in their Wranglers and boots with their caps pulled low and earnest over their brows. Only the boy who had driven stood still by the front wheel well and leaned against the van, keys dangling from a crooked finger that appeared to have been broken and never properly set. When Aloma stood by the van door waiting to be handed a pile of posters, she stole a look at him, but he was already glancing sideways at her and she thought that was wicked and could not help but like it. When she walked back into the building, a WHERE'S THE BEEF? poster balanced on her forearms, she wondered if he was looking at her from behind as she walked away and if she'd turned around, she would have seen that he was.

Inside the building she stood with her back to the auditorium door, biting her nails and eyeing the presentation on nitrogen and manure, but really thinking about the boy and his sideways glance. She looked around at the tiny auditorium, at the students with their young eyes cast up at the Aggies with their placards. Then she bit one nail to the quick to hurt herself properly, startling herself into action, and she slipped out the main door. He was still where she'd left him, leaning against the van, only now his head was lowered a bit against the midafternoon sun. He looked bored. He was blue-eyed and common-faced, not pretty.

She walked over to him, tried to look casual.

How come you're not in there with them? she said.

How come you're not? he said and she looked down quick and toed the pavement with her old tennis shoe. When she said nothing in response, he said, I ain't much for that sort of thing. They work their mouths a whole lot. They mess around. He waved his hand once.

Well, yeah, she said.

What's your name? he said.

Aloma.

He smiled at her then and she smiled back before she could think of a reason why not to. My name is Orren Clay Fenton, he said and she liked his bookless voice and the way his vowels clung to the back of his throat.

What sort of name is that?

England names. All the Fentons got names like that. I got a brother named Cash, Cassius Linus, he said. He watched her. How old are you? he said.

Twenty next week.

He smiled again and she saw he already had wrinkles around his eyes even though he couldn't be much older than she was. She wondered if he could tell that she didn't know anything about anything. With one hand on her hip, she breathed in and looked up like she was looking at something just beyond his head, the weathered skeletal shape of the trees or the blue sky, and then she sighed.

Well, I got to go back in, she said. It was good talking to you.

But we ain't hardly talked yet.

She gave him a look that had no meaning

other than to look at his face again, but he divined something there that he liked, because he said, What if I come back?

What's that mean? she said and her hand unhooked from her hip and hovered birdlike at her side.

He tipped his cap up on his head and then, as if suddenly remembering it was there, he took it off and passed a hand through his band-pressed hair. His brown hair shone reddish in the sunlight and it reminded her of the flank of a brown horse her uncle's neighbor had owned, the way the sun petted it as it moved its weight, rubbing its sides on the wood of the fence, first one side, then the other.

What if I come back and took you out?

Took me out where?

I don't know. I ain't from here. Wherever you want to go to.

I'm not from here either, she said.

Well, that's interesting to know, but that ain't a answer.

She laughed.

Maybe, she said.

Come on now, he said.

She eyed him straight then and unsmiling like a boy would and she saw the yellow edging the iris of one blue eye. Well, suppose I say yes and then you don't come back? I'd be smart just to wait it out and see what you do. That way I don't have to play the fool. Still she did not smile, but she turned her head side-ways, offered him her profile.

He grinned and propped his cap back on his head again. Then he took a cigarette out of the breast pocket of his tee shirt, watching her, and one finger fished for matches in his pocket. He found none there and so he just stuck the cigarette lightless between his lips and a tiny twig of tobacco fell from its packed end. She took a few steps back toward the school without really turning from him. He watched her dance back a pace and he shook his head. I'm coming back, he said.

When?

Soon's I drop these yokels off, I'm coming back.

Tonight? she said, incredulous.

Hell yes, tonight, he said. I can see you ain't nobody's fool.

$$\star \quad \star \quad \star$$

He did come back, and he came back again every other day after that. When classes were over in the afternoon and he was freed from work on the college farm, he showered, combed his wet hair, and tore through the three counties that separated them. He took her out in his truck as the sun was going down, and because he didn't know where he was going and neither did she, they went nowhere in particular. They just drove and he told her how big a farm he was going to own someday — bigger, much bigger than the one he had grown up on — and how to cut the testicles on a sheep and brand the hindquarters of a cow and she told him how it was to play a piano for a room full of people, to commit reams of music to memory. She liked the way he was silent and attentive when she talked about the piano, as though she were telling him about a country he had never seen. He nodded his head, his lips pressed together, and she studied his face like a score. But when she spoke, she could not really hear her own voice, but only imagined what all lay behind the press of those lips. And when the night grew late, they drove down the mountain roads to the blackened campus of the settlement school, where instead of dropping her off he parked his truck and the instant he took his hand from the steering wheel, before she could know what that hand was going to do, she scooted over and practically straddled his lap. She did not know what gave her the nerve. She'd never done a thing but kiss a boy once after a community dance and let him sneak his hand up the length of her shirt, but it took his hand forever to get where it was going and then, like an exhausted runner, it had collapsed on the finish line and didn't move but only cupped one breast. Orren's hands had considerably more endurance.

Does this mean I can come back? he said after they had kissed for two hours. She nodded, but they did not stop until the birds called for dawn.

He came back again and again and they took their drives into the mountain darkness. It was not more than two weeks before their kissing gave way to nakedness and her body gave way to his. When he pushed up inside her for the first time, she was unable to move for the surprise of it, not because it was unexpected — she had anticipated it in the unthinking way the body has of presuming its physical destiny — but because it brought the fact of Orren into a proximity she had not previously imagined. Within, but without at the same time and his face more open and more unreachable than she had imagined a face could be. It moved her in a way that had nothing to do with pleasure. That and the way, when he was inside her and reaching and speaking into her hair, he made cuss words sound like praise words. She took for the first time an understanding of what it meant to have pleasure bound up in pain, like a gift in paper. And when there was pain, which there was at first and occasionally after, she was always surprised that she did not want to end it, as if her body knew to push through any hurting for some goal that she could not understand but knew to be there. The goal was not Orren himself, though she wanted him; it was something that she could strive for only through the striving of his body, his body which she held inside her, accepting it sometimes hurting and sometimes not.

They continued on through the chilly nights, through a spring and a summer, then on again into the winter months. Ever driving and ending up parked in a dark corner of the school lot, ever compelled to strip away their clothes without regard for the cold. She told him that she would someday get out of the mountains to study piano and he told her again and again of the farm he would own and if these two strands were like roads that could never converge, neither Aloma nor Orren cared to notice. They tangled, their bodies threshed of clothes, their mouths open to the other like the mouths of baby birds and in their meshing, they did not think about time and they did not think about difference.

Even the night when they almost went sideways into the Slaughter, Aloma did not think about it. They were swooping around a bend where the road fell off into the icy branch of the North Fork when the truck fretted to the right and began to swing out where the road was not and she saw sidewise the tremor in Orren's body as he tried to right the trajectory of its path and was barely able to. The truck juddered to a stop and when Aloma looked down out the window on her side, all she could see was the black swollen creek foaming white and no blacktop or dirt at all.

Out, out, Orren said and he threw his door open fast and before she knew what was happening he had pulled her out of the cab by the waistband of her jeans, jerking her clean past the steering column over the seat still warm from his body.

Holy shit, he said and pushed her behind him. She wasn't alarmed, she didn't have time to be, her vision was filled with the living shape of Orren's back and the patch of skin between his collar and the short hairs at the nape of his neck. She laughed for a split second behind him, fearless. Then Orren walked around the rear of the truck, gazing down at the black water, and she sobered, saw with her own eyes how close the tires had come to the edge. Orren shook his head and pressed the left back tire with the toe of his boot. Then he pointed her up to a hillock with one hand and, with the other, patted the tailgate as if to soothe it. He said to her, Set yourself down and let me fix this. Aloma turned and walked to the other side of the road, which represented the road-end of someone's corn patch. In the dark she could see the shagged corn stalks, close to the ground, casting ragged shadows. She sat down at their harvested edge and watched the road.

The truck wobbled as Orren pulled it out onto the relative safety of the blacktop. Then he proceeded to set his blinkers and jack up the frame to change the tire. He lit a cigarette and knelt at the wheel well, glancing up once and again in hope no one would come wilding around the bend. When eventually a car did come, he stood up and held out his hand to wave them on, and Aloma saw him lit up by the briefest swinging stage lights, his shadow cast like a giant behind him. From where she sat up the little hillock, she could just barely see in the distance the dim lights of a house behind her, too far to matter. Below her, the road curved away to the left and right, swallowed by the black gaping of clustered trees. The horizon was close. Two hundred yards away, the earth draped down sheer from the hills to the water's edge. The hills choked out the eerie lightness of the night sky that lay beyond. But up above the highest line of trees she could see, on this chilly and very clear night, Orion in his slow-motion fall to earth. She looked down at Orren, at his curved back and the cigarette smoke that curled darkly away from his figure, and she thought how beautiful he looked, and how permanent.

Orren! she called.

Huh, he answered back.

Someday I'm gonna be a great piano player and we're gonna get out of here, she said. One finger pointed down at the earth beneath her as she said this.

He looked back over his shoulder at her and she could see the small red spark of his cigarette, but neither his eyes nor his expression. He only nodded and then turned back to the tire, and the force of his hands and the force of his young body jolted it into place.

★ ★ ★

Aloma wore a long white nightgown, one she bought from the pages of a catalog when she learned she would be coming to the farm. She stepped out of the bathroom and walked down the hall, but hesitated at the bedroom door. Orren lay in the bed facing the window, beyond it stretched a long black pasture of sky. When he heard her at the door, he rolled onto his back and gazed at her. They had never slept in a proper bed together in all the time they had known each other, a year and a half. The back of the truck on top of scattered bits of hay and crumbled dirt was the closest they ever came to stretching their bodies full length.

You look good, Aloma, Orren said.

Instead of moving, she rested one hand on the risen plane of the doorjamb and placed one foot on top of the other, the dust of one sole colored the other. She looked at him on the bed, no shirt and just his jeans. She couldn't say now why she'd thought him diminished in his body when it was clear he'd gained weight working outside. Now his darkness contradicted the white sheets. She looked away from him watching her.

Was this your room? she asked, looking from side to side.

It was theirs, Mama and Daddy's.

Oh. It was a silly question, she saw that now. Lace curtains hung on either side of the eight-paned window, the skinny moon situated in one wavy-glassed pane. And though the furniture was old and heavy — walnut greasy and black with age — small crystal and glass baubles dotted the room, knickknacks only a woman would have chosen, someone who wanted to turn a hard thing soft. Caught in the moonlight, a small glass horse reared its lambent head on the dresser, one leg forward, cantering. When Aloma moved her head slightly, the light stuttered on its hard mane and flared.

Come over here, girl, Orren said, patting the bed beside him.

She trailed forward into the room then, but stopped once more by the dresser where the horse gleamed. A photograph of Emma with Orren's father stood on the dresser top along with old receipts and Orren's keys and billfold.

Your mother was pretty, she said. Emma was smiling, her orange lipstick matched her lily-printed shirt. Her eyebrows were arched and perfectly penciled.

I should've met her. Cash too, Aloma said. I wish you'd brought me up here before now. Her fingers passed over the glass, momentarily obscuring the rounded lineaments of Emma's face. When Aloma looked back up, Orren had laid his head down, facing the window again. She stood, chewed her lip, and took one more long look at the picture. She padded over to the side of the bed and sat down and the mattress gave under her. She sat transfixed for a moment, looking down at the wooden floor as if there were something written on it that she was trying to cipher, then she lifted her nightgown over her head and lay down naked on her back. The air was cool on her skin. When Orren didn't move, she said, Do you think she would mind us sleeping in here? She braved a glance at him then. He was looking past her face out the window. And on his face was a poverty of expression that caused her pulse to quicken and she wished suddenly that she had not taken her nightgown off and actually thought to put it back on, but instead she rolled over on her side, in the same position as Orren, and looked out the window into the dark. There were at least six inches between them.

That moon is barely there at all, she said. He said nothing, he just lay there. She wanted to reach back her hand, but she only pressed it to her clavicle. Something unfamiliar rose up in her and it stuck in her throat like a homesickness, but she had no home, it was a longing that referred to nothing in the world. With a start she reached back then and grabbed his hand and brought it to her left breast so that the nipple rested in the crook of the first two fingers on his clay-brown hand. There they lay for more than a minute, breathing, the space preserved between them.

Then he slid up against her, barely moving at first like someone waking from sleep and then arranging her legs around his and pushing into her from behind and pressing her down into the mattress so that she took all of his weight and it was hard for her to breathe. To be under him hurt her breasts so that she almost spoke up, but then thought better of it and reached around to gather him in, and she shut her mouth.

★　★　★

She walked naked from the bathroom in the morning, down the hall into the room now bright with the day. Orren had risen and left with the first sun. She'd gone back to sleep and only thought later that she should have gotten up with him and made him coffee and breakfast, because that's what a wife would do, though she was not his wife.

She sat naked on the edge of the bed for a moment and pattered her feet, mulled what she should do. Her big toes left a row of wet thumbprints on the floor. When she looked up, Emma was still smiling from her photograph with a curious power, her eyebrows arched, but whether in question or happiness Aloma could not say. She stood abruptly and pushed the curtains wide. Dust

34

piled on the sills, dust that clung to the bubbled pane that flowed thick to the sash. Grassed land waved beyond it. Light refracted across her breasts and lit the rhinestone droplets of water on her legs and again she felt the small alien power of the photograph and thought to cover herself. She dressed quickly.

Aloma made her way to the hall where she found, in the closet, a few buckets and a broom, a mop, sponges curled and grayed with dirt. She kicked the braided rugs from the bedroom into the hall and with the broom she cut great swaths and arcs across the dusty floor. To the picture, she said, I am here now, like it or not. But she polished that too with the hem of her cotton blouse. She peeked inside the bedroom closet, but all that remained were old shoes. She considered throwing them out, but she remembered the emptied look on Orren's face the night before when he had gazed out past her into the dark as though she had been only accidentally there. It pricked at her mind and she left the shoes where they lay in crackled useless pairs and shut the door. She stripped the linens from the bed, noting the whitish marks that they had made last night, and she had a low, queer feeling that she had spent her wedding night without a wedding. It gave her pause, she stared down at the bed, but then she balled up the sheets and threw them aside and abandoned her campaign in the bedroom for another room in the house.

The next door in the hallway was a linen closet, empty. Then a bedroom with two twin beds, the boys' room. She hesitated for a moment at the threshold and then stepped inside and the floorboards groaned. The room had been closed for a long time, she inhaled the talcy scent of old wallpaper glue. The walls were ringed in pennants from the central college where both the boys had gone, Cash five years before Orren, so that he was back on the farm and in fact the one driving that day when the truck in front of theirs broadsided a station wagon and flung its load of sheet metal with all the force of a train into the cab of the truck so that he was crushed and Emma decapitated all in an instant. He had been an Aggie too and their miniature John Deere tractors stood parked, their tops floured with dust, sides aged blackish green on the two dressers that stood between the narrow beds. The beds were made and tightly cornered, the wool blankets sunbleached near the window. Aloma coughed and the dust motes circled in a wake. She crossed the room to the window, and after she unlatched the hasp, she still had to pound the frame with the butt of her hand before the old window loosed in its casings and gave grudgingly up. The outside air was warm and sudden and it startled the room with the smell of living things.

Out the window, far down in the lowest field, she saw Orren. His smallness surprised her, he was just a speck in the cup of the bottomland. It was not really a large farm, but it was a great deal of space for one man to possess.

As she leaned down to peer through the screen, her hand came to rest on a photograph in a frame balanced on the little bed stand. Orren, seven or eight at the time of its taking. She held it up to the light. Water had found its way inside the photo and rumpled its glossy front. It was taken in this room, the boy Orren sitting on the bed and grinning like a savage, one front tooth missing, the other chipped.

She looked around at the foreign artifacts of the room — tobacco leaf posters, puzzle dinosaurs, horses and trucks forlorn on a shelf — and all of it struck her as strange, the tokens of an unknown boyhood. She herself had no proof of having been a child, nothing imbued with the patina of age. She had packed up her life into two boxes the size of egg crates and they held mostly her scores.

She looked again at the picture of him as she replaced it on the bed stand, the small flush unlined face smooth as an ironed sheet, keenless eyes. In that face gathered the nascent force of his life, his other life, constituted mostly of the time before her. She backed out of the room that belonged to a boy she didn't know and in her mind it became tangled — what she did and did not know about the man or the boy called Orren — so that when she shut the door, she did so with a brute clap.

She hurried down the stairs into the open space of the main room. But here the piano waited for her. She touched the top with one finger, careful, as if it could crumble under the force of her small hand. She opened the cover and pressed a white bone key. There was no sound, just a sponging broken depression. She pushed down the neighboring keys and the pitches yawed out, one string buzzed hideously. She stepped away suddenly and looked around herself as if seeing the room, the house, for the first time.

Shit, she said and put a hand up to her mouth to cover it and keep it from uttering another word. She was alone in a strange house that did not belong to her. For a long time, she could not bring herself to uncover her mouth. She blinked a few times. She put her hands on her hips and resolved silently that she would say nothing about the piano, that she would not be foolish, not be lost. Then she began to clean in earnest, and once she started, she could not bring herself to stop for three days.

★   ★   ★

On the third day, when she'd grown sick of the smell of linseed oil on her hands and even sicker of the meals she'd made in a single skillet using the foodstuffs from her one trip to the grocery, she caught Orren late in the afternoon. He had just come around the front of the house with an auger flighting up in one hand and chicken wire in the other, rolled and tied. He did not look up until he almost ran into her. She said, I need things from that other house, Orren.

He shifted his weight from one foot to the other and looked down the slope at the small house, the chicken wire graded so it rested on the ground between them. How come's that, he said. He did not look pleased.

There's not hardly anything to cook with, she said. How do you expect me to feed you if there's nothing to work with? Why don't you drive me down there.

He shrugged once, but he nodded. Yeah, he

said and continued on around the back of the house where he laid his tool in the bed of his truck and the chicken wire at once sprung loose from his hand and uncurled itself. Orren pressed up the tailgate until it caught and he pulled his keys from his rear pocket.

But he did not come into the house with her. When she slid out her side of the cab, he remained where he was behind the wheel. He took his cigarettes from his pocket, thumbed the lid free. Take what you want, he said. It's unlocked. His finger tapped the white butt end of a cigarette.

The door gave way to the smell of must. The house had not been opened at all, at least she had never seen Orren down here. He was in the fields whenever she looked out the back door for him, or by the barn in the morning scattering scratch for the chickens, letting loose the cows from the rood pen. But this dank little house, into which she walked with its low fluorescent lighting and cracked louvered blinds, this he had not touched. The windows were all closed, they had died on a cool day. One by one, Aloma unhasped the windowpanes and pressed them up as high as they would slide in their painted frames. It was better for a house to smell like cow shit than like something forgotten. Then she drew open the kitchen cupboards and in their

40

recesses found all the utensils Emma had used for her cooking. Aloma discovered a box under the sink and she piled in everything she could use until it brimmed over with skillets and cutting boards, spatulas with the tiniest fragments of unwashed egg adhering, glasses with blue roosters on them. She looked behind her at the darkened hallway that led to the bedrooms. She raised the hem of her shirt to wipe her upper lip and took unfeeling stock.

As she stood there, Orren came up behind her. What do you want me to carry? he said.

She pointed to the box, but looked at him. He stood beside her, straight and plain as a cooling board.

I do like this house, Aloma said.

Orren shrugged. Small, he said.

But it's so much nicer down here. It's modern, she said, turning toward the hallway again.

Well, the old house is cooler, he said. You'll thank me come July. And then he added, as if in answer to a question, I was born in that house. And Aloma, feeling there was nothing she could really offer in response to that, said only, Oh.

Orren reached over then, and in a gesture that she recognized from the day she arrived, one that was new in its filial reserve, he patted

41

her on the shoulder the way he might touch a stubborn animal, and she pulled away suddenly, turning her face. She blinked away the play of feeling on her features. But his eyes were not on her, they had not left the dim low hallway and the closed doors there. She left him where he stood, staring with his arm still partially raised, and walked out empty-handed into the sunshine. She leaned against the raised tailgate, waiting. Beyond the truck, the cow pasture fence flanked one side of the house. Tall bluegrass bearded the posts of the fence where otherwise the grass was short, mown low on the one side, grazed low on the other. Her nose found the green scent of grass in the midst of the manure, hay, hoof-churned soil, the heated mechanical oiled smell of the old truck — all of that mixed in the nerved air, none of it familiar. She lived in a place where nothing reminded her of anything and all that had come before was unknown. For her, the land was starting. And though she had known Orren for a year and a half, she fidgeted now with the dawning sense that perhaps they were only starting too. She remembered the first time he'd spoken of marriage. He'd said one day, You gonna be my wife or what? and she'd made a joke of it, said, Sure, but don't get too stuck on me — I'm not long for this place. His eyes had danced and then he winked at her and only later it disconcerted her, that wink; it seemed to make a fool of her, or it rendered her a little girl suddenly, all aspiration and no plan. And no will to execute a plan if she had one. She thought back to their late-night rides and she divined now the many unspoken rules of engagement she'd been ignorant of at the time. Perhaps her ignorance had been unremarkable, even common. She chewed her lip.

Orren walked out of the house with the box in his hands and they slid into the truck and as he was cranking the ignition and pushing into first, she looked at him furtively, trying to reconcile the features she saw in front of her with the boy's face from the photograph in his old room, the boy grinning without reserve. He felt her staring at him.

What? he said.

Nothing.

He shrugged and then his hand weighted on the right side of the wheel and the truck carved the dust toward the house.

Hold up a minute, she said and she placed her hand on the wheel lightly to stay him. He braked, looked over at her. I haven't really seen the place yet, she said.

Don't let's do it now, he said. My stomach thinks my throat's cut.

Come on, Orren, she said. I live here now, I'm not visiting. I'd like to at least see where I live at.

He looked over at her with his blue eyes and for a second it seemed that he was considering something that was vaguely troubling to him. Then he said, Yes ma'am, and cut the wheel with both hands so the axle complained and the cab tilted like a boat on water. He drove the truck down past the stock barn and the cow pasture. The barn itself, painted a deep and decaying red, looked to be in mid-shudder with its rough boarden sides loosing from its crib frame.

That barn must be about a hundred years old, Aloma said.

No, he said, not near forty. It's a third barn. The first got burnt down by sympathizers that come around the ridge burning crop barns and then my granddaddy tore up the next one when one of the rafters fell in and killed his horse. He built this one all crookwise, put that calf gallery on the early side.

Oh, where are the horses at now? she said, casting back over her shoulder into the shadowy interior of the barn where the stalls were piled with hay or tools but otherwise barren. A few chickens looked drowsy and shipwrecked by the wide door.

I sold em, he said.

What? When?

The day after the funeral.

What for? she said.

For cash, Aloma, he said and he punctuated his words with a hard look. They drove on and the cows turned to watch as the truck passed. One cow, her belly swollen and low, swung a gentle heavy head and stepped once in their direction. Aloma half turned in her seat.

That's the fattest cow I ever saw, she said.

She's pregnant, said Orren. And Aloma barked out pure laughter at herself, but because Orren did not join her — and he once would have, she knew that as she sneaked a sideways glance at him — it sounded hollow, like her mouth was echoing a joy that had already passed. She settled back in her seat and looked away from him and the barn. She tucked her left hand between her legs and pressed her knees tight together. With her right hand, she gripped the door where the window rolled down and touched the dust that sanded the vinyl and the chrome there. When she withdrew her hand and looked into her cupped palm, the dust clung to her. There was dust on her shirt, on her face.

Tobacco, said Orren, looking past her and

45

she followed his gaze.

I know it, she said, her voice husked out in a whisper.

It ain't much, he said as if she had not spoken, but you don't need much. It sells pretty high. Corn out to the ridge, he said and he pointed out past the steering column to the field of corn that touched the skirt of the ridge as it rose out of the tilled bottomland.

She looked over the tobacco. The plants' lower leaves splayed wide from the skinnier tops, but they were not tall and the leaves, though green, depended slightly from the stalk in early, unnatural declension, a weathered anemia she saw when they drew close. Beneath the flagging breadth of the butts lay the tanned face of the soil — not an Indian red, but a pale color paupered by the sun.

They look kinda puny, she said.

It's too goddamn dry, Orren said. If I make a buck this season, I'll transplant into that field next year, and he nodded toward a fallow field that lay to the south, she could just see its bare face beyond the tobacco.

The thing is, I only want . . . he said, but then his sentence closed down unfinished. He grimaced out at the fields and she saw the deep elevens etched between his eyes, eyes

46

that were the color of the sky and just as distant. He looked to her like a thing seized, as if all his old self had been suckered up from his body proper and forced into the small, staring space of his eyes. She did not like these new blinkless eyes of his and she did not like the way his words all collapsed in his new way of talking. As if his tongue could not bear the weight of words any longer. Or the person beside him were not there.

Orren brought the truck around the far end of the fields, under the upsweep of the rising, wooded ridge and then back around the cornfield so that they came upon the house from the east. They said nothing further and Aloma watched as the house grew larger and whiter, its disuse and age arriving in higher and finer detail as they approached. Orren drove up the slope and parked behind the house so the late-afternoon sun stoked a fire on the windshield and Aloma had to close her eyes before she said, Well, I guess I better cook us something. Orren's only response was to help her carry the box of kitchenware into the house. She didn't know what she was going to cook and she didn't know how to use the mixers and casserole dishes they'd brought up, but she would learn. As she was hanging the pots and pans from the hooks on the walls, Orren set off away from the house, his cigarette answering momentarily for his presence before it too faded, and in a minute or so, she heard the tractor start up and move away out of her hearing. She eyed the empty kitchen and set to work until it was dark.

★ ★ ★

Aloma had never cooked, but she did not complain. She unearthed a cookbook in the old kitchen pantry, cleared it of its dust, and forged ahead and when she made her first honest meal — the noodles underdone and the chicken tough as jerk — and Orren did not comment, she took it as the compliment it was not. She grimly assumed the duties that were hers, all of which confined her to the house. She had known that this would be part of her life on the farm. She had known without seeing it that when Orren said, I'm taking the farm — and not auctioning it, not selling it off, not even taking anyone on right away but doing it all himself to keep costs low — it would be a great deal for the two of them to handle. And she knew that she would have a house to run, but she'd hoped it would be the smaller house. He had told her of it that very first night when he'd described the farm. He had told her the old house was falling down, the one built by his great-great-grandfather, which his mother had moved out of when Orren was a little boy, only two months after his father died. The house was more than Emma wanted now that she had a farm to run, where before she'd only chased after little boys, and suddenly she was all over the land from the sewing to the bundling, the fencing, the cows and the horses. The only thing she never learned anything about was the machines, and when they broke, she would always shoo the boys away. It was years before Orren realized that she sent them off because she did not want to cry in front of them. Pouring money into machines she ought to know how to fix tore her up. He laughed when he said this, leaned his head back on the seat and looked up at the cone top of Spar Mountain, smiling. She could be right tough, he said. That's about when I quit riding horses.

When? said Aloma.

When I was seven, eight maybe. Right not long after Daddy died.

Why's that? Aloma said.

Two things. One, this old bitch hoss run me out into the pond once, it was pretty deep, and kept me there till after dark and I was too scared to get down and wade my own self out.

49

Oh no, she laughed.

Alligators. He grinned. But Mama found me. She was mad as hell at me and that horse too. I don't think I never touched that horse again. And two, that's about the time when it was just work. We always done chores before, but when Daddy died, then it was either let the whole thing go to hell or go to work. He shrugged. Mama worked the most, though. I'll give her her due.

Aloma wondered now, Had she ever worked? She had, but it wasn't the same thing, learning to play the piano. She had never been driven by the imminent loss of something like a home. It was more a matter of what she did not have than of what she could not stand to lose. She had wanted to possess something and when she wanted a thing, she wanted it bad. And it was sheer luck that she happened to be good at the one thing she wanted. The fingerwork came easy and so did the memorizing — she did not even have to try, a fact that she liked to show off every week and it both pleased and rankled her teacher, who wanted her to slow down and listen and obey the page, something Aloma could not do when she was young, she whipped the pieces into a wild spirit of her own invention. Mrs. Boyle said Aloma could make people dance at a wake. It was not a compliment. So she reined her in, talked her down, but she never touched the bold part of Aloma's brain that could seize the scores and hold them — sometimes for years without the pieces atrophying — and then release them so a roomful of people were compelled to sit up and listen. Mrs. Boyle was stingy with her compliments, she demanded a great deal, all the while watching carefully the girl who stared fixedly ahead at the piano like a blindered horse. She saw in Aloma a singular want, the fierce driving need of the dispossessed.

But during her first weeks in the house, Aloma did not think about what she wanted, she did not have time to think about the piano or its lack. She strove only to line up her wanting with the same want that sent Orren out of the house each morning and kept him there until the sun fell. She white-knuckle-washed all the windows in the house with ammonia and water mixed in a bucket, and scrubbed on her knees all the wood floors of the house with an old grooming brush she found under the sink. With linseed oil and vinegar, she shined every surface, excepting the piano, which she left to idle in the living room. In the root cellar, where she ventured with a flashlight in her hands, she found an old pie safe with a punched tin front and she was inspecting its backside when she saw the four-foot house snake that sent her scrabbling backward up the cobwebbed wooden steps to the safety of the lawn. She slammed the cellar doors down and stalked there, jittery, running her hands through her hair to rid it of remnant cobwebs.

There was no radio in the house to keep her company while she worked, but she tried not to think on it. She did not want to waver. But sometimes when she found herself chopping vegetables at the counter, as the knife tapped home on the wood of the block, her ears caught at the rhythm, or she found herself humming a tune and her fingers jolted for an instant, wanting to stretch on the keys. She would miss it if she let herself, but she was busy in the big house and she vowed to wait until the right time to speak, if her temper did not flare like a match and burn the right opportunity down.

Now in the fading hours of another afternoon, she stood in the kitchen and read the instructions on the back of a bag of rice. She had spent hours bent over the cookbook, learning to slice fatback into her greens and to collect bacon grease in empty glass coffee jars when they ran empty. Her cooking had improved greatly since her first days at the house. The kitchen was her favorite room with its high walls, its white ceiling creeped with discoloration and cracks like old hairs on a skull. The sunlight touched her in this room. Its windows opened to the south, the east, and the north. And when she faced the stove, she could not see the mountains.

With the rice water rolling to a boil, she wandered out of the kitchen through the dining room with its gold pineapple wallpaper, its curio cabinets. She did not go into the front room where the photographs stared out from their wall, she leaned against the doorjamb between rooms, uncommitted. Outside, a late light crescendoed to gold over the grasses. Light found the piano, lit its scrolled feet and the swirling and striping of its grain, brown on black-brown. In its splitting and sinking frame she saw the formidable wrack of its previous beauty. She stared at the thing. The house was silent. The crickets had not yet begun to rub. Aloma drummed her fingers onto the wood of the doorjamb and thought yet again of Mrs. Boyle and her many hours at the piano. The woman had driven her, drilled her — rapping at Aloma's knuckles with a blue-and-red conducting pencil when she was irritated with Aloma's drumming, as she called it — Are you going to play piano for me or are you going to drum in a rock band? She said the music was found in the silence as much as sound. The pauses birthed the phrase and funeraled it too, the only thing that gave the intervening life of rising and falling pitch any meaning. Without silence there was no respite from the cacophony, the endless chatter and knocking, the clattering pitches. That is what she said, chatter and knocking — though Aloma did not really believe her and she had never learned to take her time or trust to patience. It was Mrs. Boyle, so concerned with sound, who had affected her talk as well. No, Miss Aloma, can't should not sound like paint. Cain't. Can't, like pant. Can't? Can't, exactly. She'd come away from those lessons a bit altered each time — Drop those aitches, said Mrs. Boyle, drop those aitches — less the girl who had left her aunt and uncle's with stinging eyes and more the girl who was always looking outward, getting ready to leave, the girl who dropped her aitches.

* * *

She had burned the rice. The black smell reached her and she started up and ran to the kitchen where it was already crisping brown into black on the bottom of the pot. She carried the pot out to the concrete steps and stood before the fan that she'd set on a chair by the open door. The artificial wind tugged her blouse forward around her and flapped the steam from the pot. Aloma could see Orren down in the pasture with his hands up under a cow's udder, doing God knows what, but he would come soon, the westering light was growing red even as she stood, the steam spilling away from her. She had half a mind to throw that rice down to the cows, but Orren would say, Now, why you done that, the way he did every time she wasted. Her eyes narrowed at the thought. She looked down at the rice held out before her, the center was still white as cotton so she kept it.

When Orren came up, his face was rubied from a June sunburn or only the heat of the day even as it was declining away. She saw that the hairs on his arms had been bleached white. His ring finger was naked and there was coal-black dirt edged up under his nails and she couldn't remember if his hands had always been like that when he had driven down from the college in those evenings, freshly showered and shaved. She couldn't remember rightly how his hands looked then when he touched her, because it had always been dark when they bedded down in the back of the truck, or even in the cab when it was too cold to crawl into the back. Too dark to see what was what.

What's for eating? he said.

Rice and chicken.

Well, I'll eat that, he said and nodded.

Damn right, she said and he looked at her then and stepped to her side at the sink and began to slowly lather his hands with her white bar soap, all the while looking at her.

Not that soap, she said. She hunted under the sink with one hand and found a brown soap with chip granules. She handed it to him.

What's wrong with that other one?

That's for me. You touch animals' rear ends all day.

I don't hardly do that at all, he said. And that's what soap's for.

Not that soap. This soap. He looked into her eyes, first one and then the other, and looked at the soap and then took the soap and washed his hands and shook his head, but said nothing. When he was done, he held his hands up before her with one eyebrow cocked just barely, but she was already turning away and said over her shoulder, Let's eat.

She'd set the table in the afternoon as she did each day, waiting for him. He sat down and she served them both. They ate.

Orren took two bites and then he said,

Goddamn, Aloma.

What?

This rice tastes like a house on fire.

Orren!

What? His hands up before him, palms out. It does.

Aloma pushed her plate away from her suddenly so that peas and peppers spilled off one side and the peas rolled like pocked green marbles to the center of the table.

What are you so ornery for? he said.

I cooked that for you.

You cooked it for you too.

She said nothing and he folded his arms over his chest and lowered his head fractionally as if he were peering at her over glasses. What, it's only food, he said.

Well, I don't know how to do it, she said. And I think I've done pretty good considering.

Yes, he said.

I'd like some respect, she said.

Well, he said, get you some.

She did not smile. He shook his head then and though he did not smile, he looked like he might and he reached over and poked her hand once with the tines of his fork. She snatched her hand away. He said, They Lord. What is it you want, Aloma?

Whether it was the dirt still under his nails

57

after the washing or the prick of his fork, she wasn't sure, but her tongue loosed itself and she said suddenly, I want you to marry me.

He dropped his fork down and it caught the edge of the plate where it clattered. He stared at her. I intend to marry you, he said. I ain't asked you to come here to ... His mouth twisted.

In an instant, the fight went out of her. Well, I know. I was just sort of picking, she said lamely.

He watched her quietly. No. You're ill with me, he said.

No.

You're ill because I dragged you out here and not married you first. His hand curled up on the table, dark and dry like a tanned leather.

It's just how things happened. Her voice was soft, womanish.

That's right, he said. Don't attach nothing to it. You want me to marry you in a real church wedding, right? Ain't that right?

Well, she said and shrugged.

Well, don't you?

Oh hell, Orren, I don't care, she said.

Well, I care, he said and stood up and his chair squawked against the floor as it was forced back. He walked out of the room, not so much angry as purposeful, as if he'd suddenly remembered he had somewhere more important to be. She followed quick in his footsteps until she saw he wasn't leaving the house, only standing at the door with his back to the room, and she fiddled with the dishes in the sink, casting a glance over her shoulder as he removed his cigarettes from his pocket and peered out into the backyard. But she could not be patient long. Her nerves rattled within her when she didn't know his mind, and that was more and more these days. She walked up behind him.

Now you're ill with me, she said in a low voice.

No, not with you, he said, lighting his cigarette and facing out the door where the long day wound out and down. No, I just can't see how I can . . . His voice drifted and again he did not finish his sentence. Aloma bit her lip and sighed, not able to see past the block of his shoulder to the land. But she did not mind, the land only looked like grief to her.

Well, you're not mad at the farm, she said grudgingly, though it took some effort not to call it the soil, the dirt, the dust that you feel unholy bound to and that's keeping us suckled up to the tit of the mountains. But her voice was even, balanced between her want for him and her distaste for all of this that he was holding in his eyes with tenderness just now like it was a newborn.

You figure it's not right to you, he said, without turning around. A tiny wisp of smoke spun around the side of his face and touched her nostril momentarily.

Don't worry yourself about that, she said.

I got a debt to pay, by which he meant the bank loans, but she didn't know that and she said, Well, God, Orren, you could mind to pay me some attention. He turned around and looked down at her then and she grinned and took the cigarette from his mouth and flicked it out the door.

★ ★ ★

She waited until he was sweaty and spent, having made his bereaved sound against her hair, before she pushed up against his chest and said, Just about now's when I'd like to play some piano. Still half on top of her, he said nothing, but breathed heavily on her for another long moment, his belly pressing with each breath into hers, before he rolled over onto his back and sighed and righted himself. Then he cleared his throat and said, easy and even, I won't keep you. It was this new flirtless damper in his voice, devoid of any play, that she did not care for.

60

Her eyes rolled over to him in the half-light. That piano's a mess, Orren. I can't play on it.

Is that right? he said and he seemed genuinely surprised.

Aloma tugged at the sheet that he had taken with him when he rolled away. He didn't help her, but just lay there and let her pull and pull until she had a ragged corner to cover herself.

Have you looked at that thing? she said. I can't play on it. God knows how long it's been sitting there. It's falling apart.

Well, if it needs tuned up, we might could do that.

I don't think that's enough.

Well, said Orren, and then in a way that didn't sit right with her, That's all I reckon we can do.

I need a real piano, Aloma said, raising herself on one elbow so that he would be forced to see her more clearly.

Last time I checked, Aloma, that was a real piano.

Orren, I'm a pianist, she said, hissing the word. I want to get serious about buying a real piano so I can play. We always planned I'd go on and I still want to. I want to go to school.

Orren shook his head before she even

finished her first sentence. He didn't look at her, though her own stare was unbroken. We can't do that, he said, and her ear caught at his long, drawled vowel, the way it swooped in the air, and for a hopeful second she thought he would say we *can* do that.

Why can't we? she said.

Because, Aloma, we ain't got the money.

Why not? she said.

Are you being dumb with me? He looked at her straight now.

No, she said.

Goddammit, Aloma, he said and he rose up on both elbows to better meet her eyes, we ain't got dick for a nickel. I'm a happy man I can even feed you at night. I can't afford to shit, much less buy you a piano. Be reasonable.

When she made no response, he went on, softer, You know I want you to play your music, but I got to worry this farm right now. This is all I got, right here, right now. I'm fixing to get you a piano, but I need you to be still about it. Just for a while. We'll get this place going and then I don't mind to buy you anything you want. But I need you to set tight. I swear it won't be long. If you can just set tight . . .

He settled back down onto the mattress and then, as if it were an afterthought, reached out to pull her in close against him so the scent of his sweated daywrung body bit her nostrils. When he turned his face up toward the ceiling, stretching his neck just slightly so his chin jutted and hardened for a moment, she saw the lie in the way he moved, heard it in his overearnest words. He was lying mostly to himself, she was just a secondary casualty.

You thirsty? she said suddenly, rolling out of his grasp, which was too loose to hold her, and stood unsteadily on the floor. Her legs shook a little from holding his body.

Yeah, he said, but don't work the tap up here. It's rusted out.

She padded down the wooden steps into the shadowed living room. Why he wanted to live in this old place and not the new where there was light and linoleum and good well water, she couldn't say. It was as if he were trying to make it clear to a world that wasn't even watching that he was in this thing alone, that there was suffering under way for the one left alive, but that he could endure. Perhaps even endure it better the rougher it was, as if couched in the pain was the secret satisfaction of suffering. He would prolong now the sorrow if that was all there was to prolong. She walked into the kitchen and filled up a glass and, unable to quiet her thoughts, she watched the rings of light spiral the skin of her hand. As she carried the cold glass back through the front room, she stopped suddenly, her heart cramped in her chest, and she looked up. The photographs hung serried frame to frame on the wall and she did not want to walk toward them, but she did. She met their gazes, the ones she could, there were too many to count. Boys, not older than fifteen or sixteen in their uniforms, the butternut color hand-drawn, their small swords gray and toyish. A little boy, his eyes unfocused, with a tall dog beside him. And young and old women with their flat-cheeked faces and knifed middle parts, all in their black dresses. Everywhere she looked, women in black with their hands on their black Bibles or folded on the fabric of their full skirts. And babies too, their dark eyes closed or open, some of them blurred in motion, while the adults simply stood and managed themselves for the long moment of the gaping shutter. And in the middle, she recognized Orren as a little boy with his mother, father, and Cash standing around him. They posed in front of a white clapboard church. Aloma leaned in. The boys and their father were smiling, but Emma appeared to have only just looked up, no certainty of expression to be read on her face. Aloma straightened up. Perhaps it wasn't about a piece of land, it wasn't about what was expected of Orren, and it wasn't about herself, the girl he once said he would marry. A soul loves most what is lost, so it was about all of these here, even the ones long dead, many he'd never met and probably didn't know the names of. It wasn't fair. Here she was in the flesh, her flesh having just ushered his flesh into hers, but he could not rest even in her. He was bound in perpetual motion to all of them. She watched their pitiless eyes and her mouth twisted. She wanted to say, I'm defenseless before you, even if you are dead. And they wanted to say back, Yes, yes, you are.

Aloma. Orren's voice from upstairs. You alright?

She turned toward the sound. Yes, she said, lying to him out loud for the first time.

★　★　★

The days of her life on the farm took on a kind of regularity. After she rose in the morning with Orren and saw him off to the fields and cows, she continued to pick away at the house. She swept the floors and the crumbling back steps every day, mopped every other day, mostly because Orren left collects of crumbled mud as he came and

65

went. She emptied all the kitchen cabinets, brushed out mouse droppings and set traps, looking first thing every morning for newly dead mice to toss out with the trash. When she found one, she carried it ceremonially to the can and let go the mouse so it fell to the bag's bottom, its neck still pinched under the bow, its tiny lifeless paws curled gentle and loose as a sleeper's hand.

One morning as she carried the trash to the bin on the side of the house, she found the withered remains of Emma's crow-kept garden. It had suffered in the weeks since Emma's death. Black-ribboned worms clung to the remaining beans that drooped down off their short poles, and a great burst of zinnias withered into greige masses, their eyes turned groundward. Only a blue coned flower clung to its color, though the cone had dropped half its tiny petals and browned. Aloma bent down to it, but even as she stooped, a white-bellied bee alighted, its wings quivering madly, taking the last pollen from a miniature yellow heart. Then it flew away and the plant remained, it stood diminished but indifferent. Aloma thought briefly of rebuilding the garden, though she did not know how. But in the end she did not want to tend another woman's garden, she did not want to tend any garden.

Once or twice when she was bored in the evening and supper was already prepared and waiting, she went with Orren to bring in the cows. She trailed after him as he wandered through the pasture, out around the hillock of trees with its purchase of shade to where they could no longer see the house and the ridge loomed high over them, a wooded limestone wall under a rack of clouds. There the cows — the few they had — collected around the pond, most times with their straight legs stock-still in the water like peculiar cumbrous waterbirds. Orren would circle around behind them, Aloma behind him, and up he would come alongside the oldest, with its aged world-weary face situated on its slim head. He touched her behind her shoulder blades, which winged out slightly below her neck, said, Sookcow, and went on walking in the direction of the house and the barn. The cow came along after him, her rump scissoring in measured paces. Aloma kept close to Orren as the others straggled in step behind. She was still wary of such big creatures and she glanced back frequently over the bodies of the cows to make sure they didn't come too close. Sometimes she pressed Orren for information when she judged his face eased up enough to allow for it. She wanted to know how old a cow could get and how much grass it ate, whether it had a bunch of babies or just a few.

Once, after a few of these sessions, she said, And cows and steers are related how?

Walking beside her, Orren made a motion like falling asleep into his hand, tucking his chin and pressing his splayed fingertips to his forehead. But he said, Now a steer is a boy cow that's cut.

Well sure, she said.

Then she said, But then what's a bull?

He cleared his throat, looked up once at the sky. Them's the ones that still fuck, Aloma.

Oh, she said, a grin. Where are they at?

We ain't got one.

How come?

Sold it. I already got a calf coming. Too much trouble, it was Cash's thing. I don't want no more cattle but can eat up this grass. Just lawnmowers that shit. I ain't got time for no cows right now.

Then she and the cows walked with Orren to the barn where he gestured Aloma to remain outside while he fetched hay — he did not want her to tangle with his rooster — and then he returned, padding the outside troughs with hay and dried corn and turning the spigot so the well water came up cold and splashing brilliant into the concrete trough.

Then, finally, with the cows in the pen and the sun falling, he followed her with dragging footsteps up to the house so that he too could rest and eat.

★　★　★

One morning in July, as she mopped the kitchen floor, Aloma heard Orren's truck start up and when its thrumming disappeared around the front of the house instead of dropping into the field, she flung aside her mop on a wild urge and tore out the front of the house waving her arms. Orren, catching her frantic motions in his rearview, floored his brakes and the truck skiddered hard in the gravel, flung up spitting stones and dust. He'd thrown open his door and had one foot on the ground before she ran up and said, Take me with you.

He tossed back his head. Goddammit, Aloma, he said. You like to scared me to death.

I want to go, she said, gripping his open door.

Sure, sure, he said. He shook his head.

He drove across the county line and into Hansonville directly to the bank and Aloma stared out the window, her eyes clutched at everything they passed as if it all could be possessed if stared at hard enough. She was silent beside him, her mouth open slightly, her hand held tight the handle of the door. She liked everything she saw.

Once Orren took care of business at the bank, they drove back down along the main street, and Aloma's head swiveled from side to side, taking in the double-story buildings set so close to one another that some did not have even an inch of space between them, full glass windows, dates engraved above their doors that surprised her vaguely. A park with four empty swings, a mother and her two shoeless children walking there, the sun rinsed their hair with light as they moved, as the truck moved. Orren drove on past a glass storefront with the words *The Restaurant* written in curly hand on the glass. Aloma whipped back around.

Can't we do some more errands? she said.

Orren cocked an eyebrow at her.

Like go to a restaurant or something? she blurted, abandoning guile.

No, Aloma, he said. No money.

Her face wrinkled up. But there's so much I want to do and I never get to do any of it, she said and her eyes actually began to smart.

What, ain't you ever ate in a restaurant before?

A couple times, she said.

They God, he said and he hit his brakes. Are you serious?

Well, she said.

Alright, he said. That's shameful. Sometimes I forget you ain't had a real life, and he turned the truck around in the middle of the block and gunned back to the restaurant. He counted the singles in his billfold before they went in.

The inside was draped with red and white and blue ribbons. Old men sat hunched at the front counter, all in a line. Old couples in the booths and two children, a girl and a boy, ran up and down a far aisle repeating a shrill word game over and over, their voices high like birdcalling. The girl's face was inlit with an expression of almost frantic joy. Aloma watched her without moving until Orren tapped her on the wrist with one finger and pointed to the menu. She settled on pancakes. When they came, she ate them with a deliberate attention as if seeing them for the first time, lifting one to inspect the brown circled underside, using the spine of her fork to separate the two plats to peer at the holed batter.

You know, I could learn to make these, she said. Orren looked at her long and then he rolled his eyes. He ate in silence and Aloma sat opposite him with a silly growing grin on

71

her face until a waitress walked by and Orren's narrowed eyes followed her. Then it happened again. Aloma turned around to look at the tall girl with pretty skin almost the color of a pancake, Aloma thought, and who wore her apron up high and tight around the small of her waist, which made her breasts look bigger. With one bite left of her pancakes, Aloma returned her fork slowly to the ceramic plate.

What are you looking at that girl for? said Aloma.

What? His eyes focused blue on her.

I saw you looking at that girl.

He shook his head, his mouth twisted. No, he said. He looked down.

Shit, she said, her voice gearing up.

Aloma, he said. Quit.

She glared at the girl, she glared at him. Shit, she said again. Who is that?

Nobody, he said. Just somebody ahead of me in high school is all. Aloma watched, but the girl did not look over once and averted her head each time she passed. Then Aloma sat back in her booth hard so that the wood made a single hump sound on the floor, she crossed her arms over her chest.

Ain't you hungry? said Orren, who began to eat again, hunched.

No, she said and she did not touch her

food again, even flicked her finger so her nail hit the side of the plate with a ping.

You ready? he said.

She raised her eyebrows.

Do you wanna go, Aloma? he said slowly, weary-sounding.

Well, I guess I do.

Orren shoveled his last bites into his mouth, and her bite too, before he rose up and walked to the register, reaching for his billfold with Aloma at his unhurrying heels and then the figure of the girl appeared. Aloma peered hawkish around his shoulder and she saw it, she saw the girl try to slip into the back server station before Orren recognized her, but he looked up and their eyes met and the girl blushed red and hot even across the thin bridging of her nose.

Hi, Orren, she said.

He nodded and said nothing, but neither did he turn away but looked hard at her, waiting, one hand still on his back pocket touching the edge of his billfold so that half of him appeared ready to turn and go, the other to fight.

I — she said, and looked at Aloma, blinking as she saw her for the first time. I, uh, I'm real . . . I am so sorry about Cassius, Orren, and your mother too. Cash was just the nicest guy. He was so funny. Then she screwed up her pretty young mouth so that her red bottom lip protruded out in a display for Orren. Orren looked at the pity of that lip. But his own mouth did not give way in return, he only looked at her and a brevity of dislike passed through him like a shiver for the girl who would avoid him as though he were not even there, as though he were the one who had died.

The nicest guy, the girl said again into the silence and she smiled weakly at Aloma — a smile that turned down at the corners of her mouth — and turned away to free herself; she strode into the back where, because she could go no farther, they could still see her. She turned her back and looked down at her server pad.

Still behind him, Aloma reached out and edged Orren's unmoving hand off his billfold and patted him on the rump and said, Let's go, and he seemed to wake and dropped his dollars on the counter and they left through the propped-open door. The noon sun raged against the prone and passive day. In the truck, she sighed loud and said, watching him carefully, That was good food, huh?

Orren only stared at the wheel in his hands as he flipped the ignition and pushed it into reverse. Then he glanced back over his shoulder once and when he reached with his free hand for his pocketed cigarettes, Aloma grabbed them from his fingers.

Hey, he said, grasping after them.

Quit, I'm lighting one for you, she said and she worked at his lighter, her finger repeatedly rubbing raw against the roller, but it would not ignite. She snapped the thing until he reached over and sprung the lock and lit it. Looks like I'm lighting it for you, he said and she laughed and waited in vain for him to join her. She took an amateur drag, passed it to him.

We should come up here more often, she said. There's a lot to see.

Like what, he said.

She turned soldierly to her right and looked for something.

A feed store, she said, but he didn't laugh.

We'll come back, she said into the silence.

Orren peeled out onto the sweltering line of the main street so the wind came in a hot roll, plastered her hair to her face. She had no hairband and she made one trial to collect her hair at her nape, but she gave up and leaned back with her eyes closed, her body jostled slightly by the stuttery articulations of the old shockworn truck.

You better drive careful, she said. I hate it when you drive fast. She sneaked a peek at him. He tapped his cigarette and the wind snatched the ash away. His eyes were half-lidded against the wind and sun so that the landscape scumbled before him.

She leaned back and closed her eyes again, saw the pretty girl's fatted-out lip, her meaningless relation to Orren. And she saw too the frozen turn of Orren's countenance, but now she also saw the face she carried in her, his face the way it came to her every so often. The sawn lines on either side of his mouth, blue eyes, the redly dark brows. Only this time as she conjured him, some memory came clear of him and she saw him driving shirtless on a hot summer evening. His little bit of belly hung over the buttoned edge of his blue jeans. He slouched against the seat, a cigarette rolling slightly between two fingers of his left hand. She was saying something to him and he was listening, looking out. She could not hear her words any longer and she thought how funny that the first thing you didn't need was the words you said. But she did remember the slouch of Orren's spine and the drape of his shoulder, the weight of his right forearm hung easily from the wheel. He kept looking over at her, stealing glances from the road. She pointed at something out the window and then, as her arm extended beyond him but still toward him really, he broke up. Without straightening from his slouch, he tossed his head back just an inch or so and laughed so that she could see his teeth, which were not straight but all fitted perfectly in his head. She saw the knobby ridgeline of his Adam's apple and his hand stopped moving over his cigarette and was still until he had done laughing and turned his attention back to the road, but with that last little bit of smile still on his face.

* * *

When they returned from Hansonville, Orren idled for a moment by the side of the house so she could climb out before he went on down to the fields. She hesitated with her hand on the latch, considering his grave face and then the equally grave wall of the house tinted gray under a cloud. But she chose the house, it was her charge. She climbed out of the cab and went inside to chew that bitter in the privacy of her own mouth.

Inside, she wandered driftlessly, first to the front door where the land graded away under tall windbent grasses until it met the road. But the front of her world was so full of empty her eyes could find no place to rest so she walked to her perch at the back door. She watched as Orren's truck disappeared around the hillock toward the pond, its axle clanked once as he turned and then nothing.

The clock in the living room churned out its little melody and banged on its bell the hour. Something in the sound snapped Aloma from her stillness and without a second thought, she walked out the back door into the yard away from the house. The willow stood down a ways off to her right, between her and the slope that led to the first skinny rows of tobacco. There was a kind of satisfaction in the smell of the summer air. She looked around her at her new life. Orren never asked her to do a thing. He took care of the fields, managed all the animals and the barn as well, and his refusal to ask for her help rubbed her against the grain. He even collected the eggs in the morning, the simplest task, something she could do. Aloma was stirred by a sudden desire to walk down there and hunt for eggs and see the cows, the ones that hadn't wandered off into the fields. To maybe run her hands over their hides, which she'd found to be dense like a woolen rug, or to pat them on the broad space where the hair whorled in different directions between their wide settled eyes. She turned down toward the barn, walking fast, and she was light on her feet, pushing up on the balls of her feet with a new and goalless hope. She'd taken no more than twenty steps when she saw the rooster standing in front of her with his wings shouldered off his body. He stood a few meters out with his hateful bead eyes on her.

Oh, she said out loud, stopping abruptly. This rooster had gone after Orren only a week ago and torn into his right calf before Orren kicked him off and swung at him with the shovel he'd happened to be holding in his hand. The rooster had winged up off the ground a few times in spite, but finally let him be, the bird's neck working convulsively, his wattles shaking like a battle standard. Orren limped into the house, deep spur punctures in his calf, swearing he was going to pop the head off the thing the first chance he got. Well, how are we gonna get chicks? Aloma asked. Bring in a dick that's more congenial, Orren said.

But now here he was, standing before her, his head still very much attached to his body. Aloma turned around and ran with no thought in her mind but running. Behind her, the rustling wings of the rooster made a rushing sound like a woman giving chase in an old-timey dress with crinolines and hoops, rushing on. When she was almost to the steps, Aloma risked a rearward look and saw he had come too close, launched up with his wings spread and talons out, head reared, his wattle swung like a red ribbon to one side. She kicked out behind her with her right leg and caught him under one wing as he was rising, and the force of her kick scuffed him off to one side. But then she did a foolish thing and tried to jump up to the third step by skipping the first two, only it was too high so her foot tagged the edge of the crumbling step and she fell, her body riding down the height of the three steps on one leg, skin tearing away from her ankle to her thigh. She didn't have time to cry out. Blood in a rush dotted and gathered in a sudden line down her leg and she leaped up the steps again and flung herself into the house. She slammed the door and a second later felt the lesser weight of the rooster striking the wood.

* * *

When Orren came in two hours later, she was still crying, sitting in the kitchen in her underpants, the deep scrapes ribboned with dried blood from her thigh down to her ankle bone. He took one look at her stricken face.

What happened to you? He had never seen her cry.

Your goddamned rooster chased me! she wailed.

Aw, he said, he does that. But when his

mouth wrinkled up in an attempt at pity, it stopped somewhere short. She glowered, she was in no mood — and she hadn't been all day — for any determination other than her own.

It's not funny.

No, it ain't funny, he said, flattening. You are right.

Don't laugh at me then. Her voice was full of threat.

No. He shook his head.

Why are you laughing then?

Lord, calm down, Aloma.

Shit! she said and she leaned forward, staring up at him so that he could see the whites all around her eyes. I don't calm down just cause you tell me to. I stay in here every day doing what all you want and all I ask you to do is kill one goddamned rooster. Why can't you do that one thing for me, Orren?

He looked about to say something, but then eyed her and rerouted his tongue. He put his hands on his hips. I don't know. I just ain't got around to it.

But that's all I ever asked for!

Well, it tore me up too, he said lamely. A bunch of times. God almighty, what do you want from me?

Her tongue spilled. I want to not be murdered by birds! I want somebody to show me how to cook something! And I want to play piano again! I want a piano that works, one that's not ruined! The words came out so fast and so much louder than she'd intended, she looked even more surprised than he did.

Well, make up your mind, he said, his voice rising. You want a new piano or you want me to kill that goddamn rooster? I can't make high nor low of you. Orren made a move to rake a hand through his hair, but then lost the will halfway through the motion so his hand remained at the top of his head like a spigot.

Aloma sat up straight again and her voice arched. I want a piano right now, and I want you to kill that rooster right now! If you loved me, you could just do one simple thing! Her voice was losing its balance and he heard it.

Woman, he said, as if it were a full sentence and not just the single-word warning it was, I will kill that fucking rooster on my own fucking time.

Aloma allowed herself to look more wounded than she really was, and deciding it was time to make her exit, she bolted up from her chair in a huff and started angrily for the door. Except she'd forgotten her shorts were still pooled around her ankles, so she stumbled and Orren had to reach out to steady her. She pushed at him impatiently, and for a second felt a furthering wild urge to beat at him, strike him across the face and chest for having brought her here to the sorry edge of the mountains, the one place in the world she wanted to leave behind her, where nothing worked, where every last thing wasted flesh into bone. She wanted to say all that with her fists, but she kept her head about her enough to just swat at his arm once without doing any real damage so that he stepped back with his hands raised and she kicked instead with extra fury at her shorts till they flew under the table like a bird under a tree and she stormed out of the room in her underpants, her bottom shaking behind her.

★ ★ ★

That night when Orren eased into bed, she expected him to treat her like something that had just come out of the fire, still too hot to touch. And he did, at first. He said nothing. He coughed quietly, as if to himself. She heard him scratch at the stubble on his cheeks and jaw. And then, when she had just begun to relax, he slid both his arms around her and began to forcibly turn her around in the bed. She would not go easy, scraping and grabbing at the sheet until the elasticized edge lifted with a snap off the corner of the mattress and she found herself flipped around and facing him, the sheet in her hand. She brought the heel of her other hand up against his forehead and pushed his head back until he had to let go of her with one hand to save his face. But then, instead of rolling back to her side of the bed where she could show him the cold of her shoulder, she struck at the meat of his arm once and in the hollow space under him reached for his neck with her mouth. For a moment he offered himself without moving. But he had brought his own anger to bed with him and they ended up scrabbling and tangling across the bed in a way that was not so much loving as mean. And sometime in the middle of it all, she became aware of the difference that had come over them and it seared her to know that it did nothing to damper the want. She did not want to like it, but she did. She had no idea what that said about them and would not look any closer as she held him. She sensed there were things that suffered from close inspection and in its bittered pleasure this was an easy mystery to accept.

Afterwards Orren said, I been thinking. Mama's church is down in Hansonville and you might could go down there.

She waited for more and when it didn't come, she said with a sigh, To do what?

See if you might could pick around a bit on

their piano. During the day or something, I don't know. If they need a piano player, maybe.

She made no reply so he would know she was still mad. But she stored it away in her mind where she could find it again later and then she fell asleep with her back to Orren and one cold hand tucked between her tired legs.

★   ★   ★

Late the next afternoon, with the light trooping west and the heat trailing after, Orren walked into the kitchen, bringing with him the smell of old cured tobacco and dirt. He looked pleased with himself, the way he leaned back against the door when he closed it and folded his arms over his chest and just waited. Quiet, watchful.

Aloma stood over a stove of soup beans and chicken. She glanced at him suspiciously over her shoulder, took in his hint of a grin and the way he patted at his breast pocket meaningfully with one hand like he had something there, then she looked away. I'm as mean as you, Orren Fenton, she thought.

Dammit, woman, just ask, he said.

Ask what? she said without looking up again.

Ask what I got in my pocket.

She sighed. What's in your pocket, Orren?

Come here and close your eyes and give me your hand.

Hell's bells, she said.

Come on now, he said. And it was the sound of his voice — the barest crooking of humor now straightened — that caused her to turn from her position at the stove and walk directly over to him with her hand held out.

Close your eyes, he said and she did. What he laid in her hand was sharp and cool, hollowed. She opened her eyes and looked down. For a long moment she could not comprehend what she was looking at and then she gasped and dropped them to the floor where they scattered, nacred and edged with gristle, across the faded linoleum.

What'd you do that for? Orren said.

What'd you bring me those for? she cried with her hands still open before her.

His face then was a tableau of confusion and irritation. I figured you'd want em for a kind of souvenir.

A souvenir of what? Of a dead bird?

He opened his mouth and then closed it again.

Orren, my God, she said and then, in a heat, as if it explained something, My God,

Orren, I'm a girl. Her words stilted out, sputtering in exasperation. Orren's brow twisted and he looked down for a second as if he might stoop and pick up the spurs, but he didn't move. And when she knew she should have stopped, she went on: Lord, just think a little bit next time. She heaved a sigh, not knowing how he could live with her and hear the words out of her mouth and lie with her every night and yet think she'd want keepsake spurs he'd ripped from a rooster's feet. It didn't suit and she didn't know why he couldn't see it, she would never know, she would never know him.

Orren leveled her with a look then, and she felt as if she'd swallowed an ice cube whole. Suddenly she wanted to scoop up the spurs off the floor and start all over again and she even made a move to bend down. She did sincerely want the moment back, but he didn't give her the chance. He turned on his heel, tore open the kitchen door, said, Fuck you, and disappeared into the dark in a way that was becoming familiar.

★　★　★

She acted like she hadn't given his suggestion about the church a second thought, but it stuck in her mind and it rattled there. She had worked as an accompanist in the school church from the time she was fourteen, charging through the hymns every Sunday morning and boring to sleep under the tepid sermons of the pastor who led the students away from the raucous ecstasies of their mountain churching. She'd been proud of the little money she earned while still a student pianist at the school, she'd saved it up, and though it wasn't enough to send her to college when she graduated, it was enough to buy her a red truck with a spiderwebbed back window and a tailgate that wouldn't latch. She'd bought it the day after she found out she would come to the farm. Now, grown increasingly weary of the shell of the big house, her hands always smelling like onions from supper or piney almond scent from cleaning and polishing, she began to study on Orren's suggestion. If she could play on Sundays, she might have access to a piano during the week, maybe they would even give her a key. She could play again and, for once, be the one leaving the house. The least she could do was drive down and ask.

She'd seen many churches growing up in the mountains, often perched on hillsides with their graveyards falling slowly down the kudzued hills. Or in the cleavage between hills where they were washed out occasionally with rain, or slurry sometimes. Some of the nicer churches were built out of red brick, but the others were rarely steepled, their weatherboarded sides painted thick gummous white and yards kept up by the congregations so that no one passing by would ever think they didn't love God enough to manicure his creation. The ones she liked the best — she hadn't been in one since she was a child — were the holiness chapels, no bigger than a trailer, steepleless and worn, with a handpainted unschooled sign announcing the preacher. But the church she found in Hansonville, straddling the county line and facing north, was not one of these. It was a larger, but common church — simple, unmonied, white. She parked her truck out front and eyed the batten-sided structure. Only one other car stood parked there, an old one, but shiny still, with long fins that flared high over its brake lights. She eyed it as she walked around it. The front door of the church was locked. She looked at her watch and, seeing that it was only ten, considered going home to come back another time, but it would rankle Orren to waste the gas. She walked around the side of the church, peering in through the eight-paned glass, none of it stained. The sanctuary was clean and tidy in a cheap country way. She tried the back door and it gave under her hand. She found herself in the church's kitchen, where a man and a much older woman were speaking with each other over a tall butcher block. They both looked up in surprise when she opened the door, flooding the room with light. The woman held a hand up to her wrinkled face and screwed up her eyes. The man said, Can I help you, miss? His eyes were dark and plain and not unpleasant.

Oh, Aloma said, I was looking for the preacher.

That's me, the man said and his voice was far deeper than she'd expected, it sounded like it came from his belly. He said, I'm Bell Johnson, as if she would take that as proof of something. He watched her expectantly.

Oh, she said. The older woman lowered her hand somewhat and Aloma could see the suspicion bloom in her face.

Well, I was wondering if you need a piano player for your Sunday services?

No, said the woman.

I'm real sorry, said the preacher. Do you go here? I don't believe I know you.

No, said Aloma, backing out into the blinding light a half step so that she was framed there, made a silhouette.

Are you fixing to go to all the churches in town asking for work? The woman turned to

Bell Johnson midway through her sentence as if she were asking him and not Aloma.

It's alright, Mother, he said, placing his hand on her forearm.

I'm sorry, he said to Aloma, we have a piano player, a good one. I reckon she's gonna hold up for a while.

I reckon, said his mother and snapped her eyelids like a turtle, only faster.

I play really good, said Aloma, with a little bit of a smile that was directed only at Bell Johnson and not his mother.

I reckon, said his mother again.

Okay, said Aloma. Thank you, and she turned to go, but then the preacher stopped her by saying, Well, if you made all the effort to come out here, I don't care to take your phone number and name and I'll give you a holler if we need anything.

Well, alright, said Aloma and she waited while he fingered around in the breast pocket of his button-up shirt for a piece of paper. Do you have a pencil? he asked.

No.

Well, set tight for half a second and I'll fetch us one. Be back directly, he said and left the room. Aloma looked at the old woman, who seemed for a second about to smile, but it was just a twitch that went nowhere. When the preacher came back in the room, he handed her a pen and she wrote *Aloma, piano player, very good.* And then her phone number.

Well, thank you, she said, handing him the paper. He folded it carefully and put it back into his pocket. She took a few steps toward the door without turning and she waved her hand, an unnecessary motion wasted on the small space. That made him smile.

Bye now, he said.

See y'all later, said Aloma.

I reckon, said the old woman.

★ ★ ★

When she pulled back up to the big house, she parked and, looking for Orren, walked on around back without going inside. She sighted him amid the slow-growing but greening tobacco, down on his knees. She walked down the hill, her weight carrying her until she was almost jogging at the bottom. Here at the foot of the small field, she passed a wasting gaze at the plants, which looked even worse up close, not the sea of green they appeared from the kitchen. Beside her, grown tall as her hips, she could see the fragile tips of the leaves, the duskiness of the water-starved plants. She waded into one row so that she had to push them away with both hands.

Watch it, said Orren when he saw her and how she was palming the plants away from her on either side. She could tell by the tone of his voice that he had not yet forgiven her for the other night.

I am, she said. Then: Shouldn't these be taller?

Yeah, he said and swiped his sweaty face with a sweaty hand, so that he smeared dirt along his cheek in fingerpainted marks. But they got a couple blooms, he said and she saw scattered along the plants the first pursing blossoms, white in their green upstanding sleeves.

When's the last time it rained? she said, aiming hard for forgiveness.

Not so long, he said. But it's too hot. I just don't want these butts to fire up too fast, and he reached out one hand to swat at a few low leaves. Aloma saw the thick sticky hairs on their broadsides, they swayed when he grazed them with his fingertips. They reminded her of a living thing, an animal's hide.

Are you worried? she said.

No, he lied. But I'd like to hear me some good news.

I have good news, she said, standing beside him now as he kneeled. Well, not good news really.

He looked up at her, he leaned back on his

haunches, his hand down at the dirt to balance him. The sun figured behind her and he squinted and could not see her, his eyes teared up from the light so they gleamed an unnatural bright against his dark face.

I went down to that church —

What, Mama's church?

— and asked if they needed someone to play piano.

That's good news, he said.

But they didn't need anybody.

Well, he said, and he wiped his hands now on his bleached and tattered Carhartts. You never know. They might.

At least I tried, she said. I might could make some money yet.

You better make a lot, he said, grimaced, and he stood then, looked at the plant right before him, which was grown past his waist.

I was thinking . . . Aloma said, still aiming.

He looked at her.

Maybe we could go do something sometime . . . away from here. She thought of Hansonville and the road that passed the church, the road that went north and kept on going.

Bad time, he said without hesitating.

Bad time . . . she repeated.

Bad time for a good while, he said again and reached out to the plant before him and topped its baby blossom between his thumb and forefinger.

Hey, she protested.

Got to, he said. You tear off the pretty parts to make it grow stronger. And the blossom fell to the ground where it peeked out lippish from its shell, its smooth young body against the dirt. Orren nudged it under the shade of the plant with the tip of his boot.

Aloma left Orren in the tobacco and returned back up the little hill to the house. She wasn't foolish enough to expect to hear from the pastor again. She wouldn't clinch a church job by walking in off the street, she knew that much, but she could think of no other option. Never mind that she'd forgotten to mention her relation to Emma, her only real connection to the church in the first place. But she'd tried and she felt better for the effort, though she'd not put her hands to a real piano. It was nearly good enough to know that she'd been in the same building as one that might have been recently tuned. That alone cheered her enough so that when she walked up from the fields, she forgot to be disappointed in the clean, ruined house and went right to the dining room table, cleared the far end of Orren's paperwork, and piled it on a chair. She brought her big box of scores down from upstairs where she'd kept it beside the bed like a hope chest and spread the scores out on the dining table — the Schubert and Beethoven, Ives, Schumann, Grieg. The names buzzed in her mind like a struck string. Flipping them open randomly, pressing them to lie flat so the table was papered in disjointed passages from a dozen pieces. She spread her hands over the pages and turned her face toward the ceiling, her eyes closed. It was an easy thing to do, recall them to mind, shape the structure of their phrasing into her fingers. She opened more scores and piled them on top of the ones already spread so they were inches deep before she stopped, dizzied by the black notes fighting for space. Her fingers shook, her hands were starved for it.

So then she found her motion in the house and it was the motion of playing. When she dragged the rugs out to the back lawn where the laundry cords were strung near the willow, she beat them in time with a broom. She beat them in 3/4, she beat them in 4/4, and then, because she amused herself this way, she switched between the two and then broomed a 5/4 and felt the forgotten pleasure of her own abilities. It was something she had not felt in a long time, the house misered out reluctant joys. And later, when she hung the laundry, the pins seemed like quarter-note tails against the white page of the sheets. She trailed her finger down the wet cotton and thought again of all the music waiting to be played. She was standing there, a silhouette portrait against the white sheets in the morning sun, when the phone rang. She considered not answering it; not because the dining room was far but because she was thinking of her music and she did not want to move, it was so pleasing, but then she relented and ran for it. She picked up the receiver and said, Hello, and a deep voice said hello back, its timbre black and warm. She did not recognize it.

Who is this? she said.

This is Bell Johnson, the voice said. When she made no immediate response, he said, I'm the preacher down at Falls Creek. You walked in the other week asking about a job.

Oh, she said and then again, brightly, Oh.

Well, he said, that was some kind of timing, because the lady who's our piano player passed on last week.

Oh no, she said. That's terrible.

Well, yeah, she was eighty-four, bless her heart. She played for a long time with us, longer than anyone could ask, I reckon. She was here with my daddy for forever, since I was little at least, and so that's a good long time. So.

I see, she said.

So, I reckon we are looking for somebody now. She taught some gals here, but they're pretty young and we're looking to have somebody a while too. Leah never took no payment, but that's not . . . What I'm saying is that we'll pay. She never took it, but we can spare it, that's the right thing to do. We can't pay nobody much, but we have some extra. Nobody's starving under this roof.

Oh, I'm not too worried. I just want to play, really, she said, but then she turned to look out toward the southern end of the farm visible out the window, out at Orren's land, and she said, But a little bit would be good.

Alright, well, you reckon you might could come down here and maybe play some for me and whoever else is around? Just some churchy songs, just to see.

Like an audition, she said.

Well, like a audition, alright.

Sure, she said, I can come down today.

Oh, okay. That's good of you.

That would be no problem. She smiled out into the room, the light from the window finding her face.

Thank you, Bill, she said.

It's Bell.

Bell. Johnson. Sir, thank you.

Alright. Well, you come on down and we

can set for a minute and maybe you can play.

I'll be there directly, she said.

Fine, he said.

* * *

He was a bigly proportioned man. She had not remembered that. Or perhaps she'd not gotten a proper sense of it in the cramped and dark kitchen of the church where she'd met him that first day. He was waiting when she pulled into the small gravel lot, seated on the front steps with his elbows on his knees, keys cupped and catching sun in his hand. It was when he rose that she saw he was a good foot taller than her. He leaned into his hip in the modified stoop of tall men.

That was quick, he said. He crossed the gravel between them, but made no move to shake her hand, only pocketed his keys and left his hands in his pockets. She caught his smile — a warm but brief thing — and the formal way he had of bowing his head hello so that she saw the blackish curls there and the white scalp beneath like snowy ground peeking through brush.

Hello, I'm Aloma, she said. Pleased to meet you again. His mouth curved slightly, interrupted his reserve, and he seemed not to know where to look. He glanced over his

99

shoulder then, made a curious full rotation once looking around and said, I was hunting around here for somebody to give a listen, but some boys who were just here had to go up to Rocky and they took my mother. She had some things to purchase up there, so she went too. I reckon it's just us. I'm no expert, but I got a ear and I know a hymn when it's rightly played.

Okay. She nodded and held her purse to her chest, remained standing with her rear to the driver's door.

Is that your truck? he said.

Yeah, she said. She looked down at it and saw how dirty it was, streaked and spattered with the dirt of the farm. It had never crossed her mind to wash it, she hoped it didn't speak to her employability.

I used to have one like that, he said and he smiled, at the truck, not her. I bought it from one of my cousins in Glenly and spent near everything I had fixing it up and then I went and I wrecked it the first week it was road ready.

He crossed his arms over his chest, and with his arms between her and him, his shoulders dropped slightly. You know that elbow bend when you come up around by the Tarson's, and it goes like this — he snaked one hand so it took a sudden curve in front of him, his eye touched hers — and here's the big cane-brake on the one side and their house on the other, I spun it out there and wrapped it around a tree. I wrecked it good and proper. He sighed. Daddy said it was a good thing, that truck was pure vanity. And it was, he laughed. It was. He sighed and looked at her, then pursed his lips. She said nothing, only watched him and smiled. His eyes were very dark and they did not linger. He said, You live around here?

She nodded, but coughed once in lieu of words.

He nodded too, seemed on the verge of saying more, but changed his mind and said, Come inside and play a bit?

They went in through the front door. The church was white on the outside, white on the inside, with no stained glass so the high afternoon sun raged through the windows, colorless. The pews were old oak, dirty blond, their scurfy varnish flaking in the light, most with thin red cushions resting on their seats, but some not. Up front, the lectern was stationed uncentered on a landing atop three steps with a workaday upright at its foot to the right of the congregation and cockeyed so the pianist could eye both the preacher and the church. Aloma followed Bell down the central aisle on a strip of red carpet worn and darkened the color of charcoal along its middle. As if reading her thoughts, Bell said, We aim to replace this rug soon, but you know how it is. Yes, she said, as if she did. Leaning across the first pew, he plucked up a hymnal, its leaves shagged by years of use, and opened it, flipped a few pages. Aloma walked over to the piano and sat down. She pressed one key and it responded as it ought, the pitch held without wavering or bowing until it thinned and evanesced out of sound altogether. She inhaled on her pleasure and she could smell the well-used piano, its waxy wooded scent.

Bell laid the hymnal down on the scrolled rack before her. How about you just play this hymn for me, he said. If you don't care to.

She had not played in well over a month, but she did not hesitate, she felt nothing but eagerness. She took one look at the printed page and said, Oh heavens, I can play that with my hands behind my back, and she closed the hymnal. But then she peeked up at him because she heard how sure, even vainglorious it sounded, though it was the truth. Then she played 'The Old Rugged Cross' as simple and straight as she could, slowing down churchily at the end and throwing in a few dissonant suspensions for good measure. She tried not to look too pleased with herself as she played the last chord.

Well, wow, he said. You play it like you hear it.

She smiled up at him. Do you just need somebody for Sundays, or Wednesdays too?

Well, Wednesdays too, I believe, he said. But sometimes some of the boys here just pick on Wednesdays, no fiddle of course, we ain't that far gone — he laughed — but we might could use you. If you're free, that is.

I can be free.

Well, that's good, that's good. You don't got obligations elsewhere or anything? he said, his eyes turned up to the window behind her that lighted her, burning the edges of her brown hair blond.

Nope, she said.

Okay, he said. Well, wow, that's great. He looked around the sanctuary for a moment, his eyes searching out the front door that they had left open so that the July day penetrated the cool of the sanctuary. Aloma saw the small beads of sweat on his forehead, and when he put his large hands on his hips, she saw the sweat rings on his shirt.

As he gazed out over the empty pews, he seemed to think the better of his haste. You don't just got that one memorized and that's the only one you know, right? He smiled shakily at her.

She laughed, let the hymnal fall open where it would and she played one verse of 'O Come, All Ye Faithful.' He laughed too as he listened, and though he kept, his arms crossed over his chest the whole time while they were speaking and laughing, she was pleased, and when he offered her fifteen dollars a week, she felt even better. And she thought, Orren will be happy, and she liked that.

When she stood up to go, her face was pink with pleasure and she looked more beautiful than she was. Bell unfolded his arms just long enough to grasp her hand finally with his own oversized hand.

Well, I'm pleased to offer you a job, he said.

I'm pleased to be playing piano again, she said. It's been a little while.

Oh, how come is that?

Oh, she said and shook her hand in the air, conjuring. It's just been a while is all. I'm rusty.

Well, you can play here as much as you need to, he said.

That's about the best news I've had in a while, she said.

Well, good.

Good, she said and laughed again.

When she came home, Orren was walking up from the barn with something hanging from his right hand.

Guess what! she yelled from the back steps.

What? he yelled back.

I got a job playing piano at the church!

Paying you? he yelled.

Fifteen dollars a week, her voice a little softer now as he neared. He said nothing in response, only kept on, and that stole the slightest pleasure from her telling. As he topped the slope, she saw he was carrying a dead chicken, its head gone but its body still whole and feathered. She stepped out cautiously now to meet him on the grass.

What's wrong with that chicken? she said.

It's dead, he said. She glared at him.

It don't lay no more, he said. It ain't a meat chicken, but we can eat it. Fix it, he said and he held it out to her. There was fight in his eyes, and because it was there and because he hadn't forgotten the other night and neither had she — especially the part where she wanted to take back her loose words — she reached out and grasped the chicken by its nubby legs and held it right up against her hip so her jeans got wet from its spillage. She didn't know what to do with it, chicken from the grocery was one thing, but holding the deceased in her bare hands was another thing altogether.

Fifteen bucks, huh, he said.

That's right, she said and smiled broadly. Then she turned and walked back to the house, swinging the chicken like she didn't care.

★ ★ ★

On Sunday morning, she woke and Orren was still in bed beside her. Her eyes found the clock, there were two hours remaining before the service. She lay still for a few minutes, aware of the sun and its increase and the unfamiliar fact of Orren's easy sleep beside her. But when she made a move to rise, he startled her, he rolled over and laid his body over hers. His head remained burrowed down in her neck as though he were still asleep, accidentally on top of her. She pushed up once at his chest, but he didn't move.

Are you going to do something or just trap me? she said.

When they were done, he rolled back to his side and rested again. She looked over at him lying there with one hand on his chest, loose, his eyelashes drifted down.

I don't think you should go with me to church, she said.

He opened one eye and peered at her. Did it look like I was fixing to go?

Well, I'm just saying, she said. It'd be better if you didn't.

Why? he said darkly and opened both eyes now.

Don't be ill, she said. It's just that they don't know I live with a man and it's better if they don't. The preacher didn't know it when he got me to do the playing, so it would be better —

I get it, he said.

I'm not mad, she said. It's nothing about that. It's just, they don't need to know.

Well, I don't go to church.

I noticed, she said disapprovingly.

I don't need nobody to bitch at me, he said, shutting his eyes and raising his hand to cover them.

Okay, she said and rolled her eyes and sat up in the bed, one arm holding her breasts while she looked around. Her hair stuck up in the back. You knot up my hair, she said. I hate that. He didn't reply, but a minute later, while she was rooting through the closet for a dress, he said, The singing I don't mind, but I can't abide nobody telling me what to do. Shit. I went when Mama made me, but never again. No, buddy.

They're only just making suggestions, said Aloma with a dress now in her hands.

Orren tented his hand and looked at her. That's the dumbest thing I ever heard you say, he said.

She ignored him. It was Sunday. She hooked her bra and pulled on her dress, turning toward him as she buttoned it over her breasts.

Are you staying in bed? she said.

No, he said. I'm fixing to work. Let those other sonsabitches go to church. I got shit to do.

★　★　★

On the drive down, Aloma's stomach was drawn tight with the edginess that came before playing, something she had not felt in a long time. Her brow creased and her right hand worried the stick when she wasn't shifting and when she finally pulled into the church's gravel lot, she had to sit still for a moment and collect herself, breathing. She'd made a point to arrive thirty minutes before the service began, but the small lot was already milling with people and she could see Bell by the front steps talking with two men. She tried not to feel very girlish and very young when she approached them and said in a voice she barely recognized for its softness, Good morning.

Morning, Miss Aloma, Bell said and the two men turned as one to look at her and she blushed and held up a hand to shield her eyes from theirs and from the morning sun, cut and shafted but not weakened by the shaked church roof.

I thought to come a bit early to practice, but I guess I'm not so early.

I don't reckon you need to practice at all. She's good, said Bell. This is Miss Aloma, the new piano player. Aloma waved at them, but did not shake hands and they did not offer. They nodded, smiling, and looking at her sideways without words until Bell said, Oh, I reckon I should tell you what we're singing.

He led her up the steps and into the church where some of the women and a few of the oldest men were already seated, their Bibles at their sides.

Now, normally I would leave this up to you, he said, but I just gone on ahead and picked them this week. I'll let you know what I'm fixing to preach on and then you can do it yourself. That's what Leah always done and it worked fine.

Alright, said Aloma, following close on his heels up the center aisle as she had the other day. A few people turned to mark their passing. She sat on the edge of the piano bench and arranged her skirt so it fell neatly from the shelf of the bench down to the threadworn carpet. Bell, his dark eyes following the movement of her hands, said, Two hundred forty, two hundred and forty-one, and fourteen. I'll let you know when on all of it. And then he smiled at her, but not long, and he turned on his heel abruptly so that it struck her as almost rude and she looked up, startled. She watched as he walked away. He stopped to pat the knee of his mother, who sat steel-backed, Bible on her lap, in the front row and then he passed on back down the aisle and out the door again to greet.

Aloma sat perfectly still, wondering at her sudden feeling of aloneness and what seemed now the oppressive quiet of the small sanctuary. She felt them watching. She averted her eyes so she could not see them at all and she ran her hands silently over the chord progressions of the hymns, her hands shaking slightly.

At five before the hour Bell came inside and he walked up to her at the piano and he was so tall she had to crane her neck back to see him properly. He said, Why don't you play a bit, to draw em in.

Oh, she said, yes, and rejolted into action, her hands trembling on the keys. But as she pushed beyond the opening bars, her fingers found their old habit of being, and the memory of her muscles drew her mind into the song. Her breathing slowed and she found once again, as she always did, that she had a fearsome control of herself at the keyboard — if nowhere else in the world. From the invitation, she ran straight into the first singing hymn and the congregation rose beside her. Then came her own shuddering response to the sound of their hollered singing, the mismatched pitches rubbing and abrading against one another, the static of imperfect voices. It was not perfection that moved her, only that rub, what others found ugly. She sought the joy of misshapen things. But too soon the clamor was over and with it the noisy anonymity that cloaked her and Bell introduced her to the curious congregation as Miss Earle. She half rose from her piano bench with a forced smile and a heated face and promptly sat back down again, looking to neither the left nor the right but straight at Bell with such intensity that, in that instant, she memorized him.

Then Bell preached. We are all lonesome men, he said and he turned his head down with its black curls, looking like a sorrowful bird with its beak tucked into its chest. And he stayed there for a moment like that, breathing, before he lifted his head again. I one time heard a man say that the human was the lonesomest thing could be read after in the world, that there's not a animal in the whole animal kingdom with sadness laid on its heart like ours, and I suspect that's true. It's a thing we're all wearied of, each the one of us, this being amongst all the people and ever being alone. Even Jesus was alone in the desert with not but a fool devil to keep him company. Bell paused, breathed, and fingered at his brow, not looking away but surveying them as he took his time. Aloma saw a brief shadow of thought cross over his features.

I been lonesome too — nobody's immune after the cradle — but I got wind of God from a good upbringing so I knew, even in my dark hour, to reach out. I called up from my earthly crying, brothers and sisters, I called up from the depths and from the selfishness of my own heart and unto Thee I gave myself, that's the truth. And grace hammered me, it was like my bones breaking, it broke me up, brothers and sisters, and it hurt. Grace don't always feel like something good. It cut up my heart. Grace'll come, but don't expect pleasure when it does. He looked out at them. See, I gave up and submitted my own self, though I didn't want it, nobody wants it, nobody wants to be a slave. The whole world is fixing to tell us one thing — Live big in the world, take up all the space a body can, feed the body, love first the body. Well, I gave up the body through grace, I gave up my own grave-drove desires though it's a constant temptation, Lord, it's a constant temptation to backslide. You know how it is. And they amened, they did know. He was sweating now, stoked like a stove before them, though there was no wildness in him, only will.

But funny thing was, when I gave up, when I submitted — that thing I wanted most not to do — I found I wasn't half so alone as I was before, even if I am just alone as ever, so far as the world considers. No, not half so alone, cause my heart was turned out like a shirt wore wrong side out, brothers and sisters, that's how it was when God turned me, so that my innermost heart was all exposed, facing the world and not my own self. That's the good thing God did when he made me not what I wanted. But I didn't do it, God did it. I didn't say, Come in — God said, I'm coming in. All I did was only let him. Yet I had to give up, I had to submit me to something I didn't want, to the will of another. That's the opposite of the world, to rub your own self out. World wants you to take up ever more space, brothers and sisters. But God asks us to be less so that others might be more.

He continued, And don't you know it, once I shut up, once I got my own voice all stilled, then I heard it. Then I heard what it was God was fixing to get me to do, which is preach, which is give. And I got lighter of the spirit, of the body, and I saw our dreams come with many cares. That's written. My dreams were heavy on my own back. And here's the thing about God when he speaks, he — Listen, God don't sound like no coal train come howling down from the driftmouth, God don't sound like heavy weather, God don't sound like God. He paused, eyed them, wiped the sweat rolling now from his brow down the sides of his face, grimaced slightly, and smiled. He said, Small, still voice, a little murmur. He held up his hand, two fingers an inch or so apart. He shrugged. I ain't made it up, it's written, he said, shaking smally the Bible. Elijah goeth up unto the mountain and in the cave he heareth the small still voice. And that was the voice of God. Ain't that just . . . And he laughed to himself, sobered, looked out at them with accusation and a fierce look like love. What do you think that voice says? He waited a moment. Submit, he said, and then a thin woman stood in the center of the church, her flesh whittled by a stingy hand very close to the bone, and she wrapped her knobby hands around the pew in front of her, leaning forward. Her hair fell like a gray curtain over her face. She rocked a little, the man beside her reached up once, patted her on the back, lowered his hands to his own withered lap. Submit unto one another, Bell went on, watching the woman, called her by the name Ellen and she lifted her hands above her head and a few more congregants popped up, hands to their chest or the air. And Aloma found that she could not turn away, not from their standing and undressed emotion or from Bell, who stepped farther out so that he was almost in the first pew and he called more of them in his rising black honey voice, brothered and sistered them by name and held his Bible up higher before him as he called them. And the rolling cadences of his voice urged them on in their own prayers, prayers that leaped from them even as he preached so that their voices joined to his in an upsurging of spoken need, until it became unclear who was preaching and who was listening, but now almost half the congregation stood in an energy she did not recognize and even as it frightened Aloma — their yielding and their babbling — she felt an uneasy joy.

Because she could not help it, she sang all week. She came home from church that first Sunday with a tune in her throat and she carried it with her all day until she lay down with it in bed, though she didn't realize it until Orren said he couldn't sleep, she was buzzing like a hornet. But she had put a hand to the piano again and she was glad for it, and if Orren didn't understand her, she could not make him. What did he care to know of her anyway, with his earthfast disposition, his increasing hours away from her? She petted herself with the idea that she would be fine without his gritting presence. Short of keeping him awake at night, he did not seem to notice the change in her. She had the feeling more and more now that his eyes looked through her, that she was like foxfire, a ghost. And even in bed sometimes she sensed that when he said her name, it was just some strange and misnamed conjuring. When he stiffened inside her and craned his body as if some fever were cresting to break over him and he had to help it or resist it — it seemed like both — with every fiber of his being, she did not always think it was really her he was calling when he called her name. But she held on to him anyway, as if she could save him

116

from his fever by clinging tight, but there was a part of herself now that she kept back.

When she trailed out to the tractor in the afternoon, taking his lunch to him so he would not have to walk in, she hymned as she walked and paced her expirations to the tempo of her feet. Orren would take the food and say thank you and never comment on her newborn singing, only eat quickly and continue on with his day, which was the fertilizing and the watering, fingering the plants with a consternation that grew as he eyed the sky and checked the weather on the radio that he kept on his tractor. He moved now with what had always been the edgy promise of his body. If he said anything at all, it was, It better goddamn rain, or as he did one time, just turning his face up to the sky and charging it with a look of hate and questioning, both.

Orren, she had said then, disapproving. And she looked around as if there were actually someone there to witness his spite, but it was just the two of them and the blue tractor and the barely budded plants and beyond them the buckled ridge of the mountains with its late greens. Orren looked down at her dully for a moment, but she stood her ground against his unnearable gaze and she inspected him. The cap pulled low, deep oval stains of dirt on his thighs and knees, and between his fingers, the ever-present white stalk of a cigarette. None of these things described a change in him, but she wondered when she had last seen him smile. She could not remember, she gave up. There was no point to remembering any-more. She only wanted Orren back, but she was no longer sure that even the rain would bring that.

★   ★   ★

On Wednesday, after the merest drizzle the night before, they woke to a whitened field. Aloma came down the steps first and almost dropped her coffee mug for the shock of it when she turned in her nightgown and saw the field of green topped with fists of irregular branched flowers, as white as the gown that swirled around her hips and legs when she turned. Orren, she called, but he was silent, still upstairs, and she slipped her bare feet into his work boots, felt the grime and deep press of his wide feet so that she felt herself for a moment to be standing in him, then half ran down the slope in the cool near-morning. The sun had not yet breached the ridge and the light of the air was white overhead, thin and unfinished, yet the coming morning burned a single thin fire line on the black ridgetop, it distended and filled like a blister with the blood of the morning even as she watched. The western fall of the ridge was black, black as its eastern side collected the rising light. The shadowed ridge crested high over the field as she ran down past the willow, its withes bowed oblivious in the still air, to the edge of the field and she stood there to catch her breath. The white bunched blossoms had breasted out of their buds overnight, coming in darkness into sudden blooms the color of morning. They massed in whiteness before her, they topped the bruised and weathered plants. The sky marshaled, deepened even as she stood there breathing and watching in wonder, it lightened as she stepped into the first row, reaching out to find a branched blossom with her open hand, the way it spread orderless and fresh over the uncomely, sticky-haired working tobacco leaves. The dirt under her feet breathed figments of fine dust as the soles of Orren's boots pressed against it. Any rain of the previous evening had come and gone, as insubstantial as dew, and the soil was dry again. Aloma turned around then, and with her hand still raised to the white tongue petals chest high, she looked back at the house silhouetted against the fading dusk of the night sky. Orren stood in the door, her abandoned coffee cup in his hand. Aloma withdrew her hand from the blossom and returned it to her side. For a long moment she contemplated his figure and the effort required to walk back up the hill and then she succumbed, she left the white field and went to him. The first orange sunray burned the eaves of the house as she stepped beneath it. In a moment, it would burn the white of her gown.

That's a mess of topping, Orren said when she drew close enough to hear. That's my task today.

What?

Top that whole field. Succor soon enough.

Aw, she said, childlike, standing beside him and turning so they both looked out over the brightening field. Both their lips twisted down to the far sides of their faces.

Can't you leave it be just a little while? she said.

Not less you want to starve.

Well, say what you mean, Orren. She sighed.

He blinked at her in surprise a moment, then cleared his throat and said quietly, We was raised to speak our minds. Mama didn't want no middling boys.

Aloma said nothing in return, only turned

to stare balefully out at the field again and he followed her gaze. It is pretty, he conceded.

White as Christmas.

Let's just make it to the real Christmas.

I never had anybody to do Christmas, she said suddenly.

Well, I don't got nobody my own self, he said, and as the unintended weight of his words settled on her, she looked at him pointedly so that he couldn't help but see his own mistake and he said promptly, Now, I ain't meant it like that. But she was already moving past him into the house and she didn't see that he turned quickly and followed her jagged movements with his eyes. She kept her back to him, tucked her chin into her neck, cracking eggs in a bowl and refusing to look back at the fields or at him. She did not want to see him against the burst of white. In a few short minutes, the smell of bacon frying drew him slowly in from where he stood sentinel on the steps. He stepped beside her to pour black coffee into his mug, though he didn't try to say anything else, he moved gentler than his weight accorded. He let her ignore him. Then he took a full plate of food and headed out without a word.

All day he kept to the fields and Aloma watched from the kitchen door as row after row of tobacco plants was shed of its white.

121

She tried to persuade herself to work in the house, but she was driftless, bored with herself, drawn repeatedly against her will to her post at the back door where she monitored the topping. And her spirit fell by increments as the blossoms went to the dust. She picked at her nails, she sweated in the doorway, Orren moved plant to plant under the sun.

When the phone rang in the middle afternoon, she couldn't say how long she had been standing there, squinting into the field, waiting for something to force her away. She recognized Bell's voice right away from its depth, its dark and pleasing pitch.

We won't be needing you tonight, he said and she felt a keening disappointment, wrapped the phone cord around one finger and said, But could I still come? He laughed then, saying, Well sure, of course. I'd not stand in the way of a woman who wants church. So she wandered down past the willow onto the plowed lip of the field where she called out a lie to Orren, said she was needed to play at the church and then she left him where he stood half-turned to hear her with a knife in one hand and sweating in the deepening heat.

In the church, she made a point to sit in the back row where this time she could cast her eyes about, freed from the gaze of others, freed from the piano. Bell wore jeans on this hot night and a short-sleeved shirt and she saw sweat rings in the blue shirt so sheer it was almost white. He towered over everyone else in the church and he drew a gaze by virtue of his height, she wondered if he knew and liked that. He grinned easily at everyone and, because it was Wednesday, spoke loosely as though he were in his own home. Three men led the singing, each with a rosewood dreadnought worn paper-thin where the pickguards once had been, and everyone knew the songs and Aloma did too, not because she had sung them in the school — they'd been disallowed there — but because they'd been bred into her in a time long before school, though they'd been long buried like a seam. She sang softly at first, almost afraid to make her presence known in the church where she felt she did not belong, but then she sang out and by the end of the two hours, that feeling had returned again, the one she'd felt on Sunday morning, a feeling that had nothing to do with God or not God, but only with a sound risen on her breath. She would have felt it if she'd sung in a field or a kitchen or a bed, and she felt it in a church just the same.

When she left, she hummed the old

modaling songs until she turned into the gravel drive, long after nightfall. The house and the fields were dark, but as Aloma stood quietly on the back steps peering into the depthless black, she could tell by the uninterrupted shadows that every last white blossom had been cut.

★ ★ ★

The next Sunday Bell Johnson preached on waking to creation. Aloma played hymns of her own choosing except for 'Come My Soul, Thou Must Be Waking,' because he asked for it especially, saying it was a favorite and that it spoke better than he could to how it was to wake and pay right attention. She did not know what he meant by right attention, but when they sang on Sunday morning, she felt their singing was indeed a rendering of all their feeble strength could pay and she could see how even the efforts of the strongest men, the ones who were broad and young, even their strength was feeble against the backdrop of the whole earth. That could not be denied, or at least she thought so in the moment when her hands charged the hymn from the piano and her eyes passed continually from the page to Bell to the people singing. And again, she watched as Bell took up his stance

124

at the lectern, wrapping his hands only momentarily around the pale wood before stepping away again, abandoning his post to stand almost among them in the pews. She noticed again the way he stopped to think while he preached, pausing to look out the window as if the light itself would revelate him. Then when he spoke again, renewed, he moved up and down on the landing as he felt led, pausing occasionally for a word, and the people stayed with him, they fanned themselves or shifted to ease their backs, but all in patience, all in waiting.

At the close of the service, when most of the congregants had wandered out to stand milling in the parking lot, Aloma trailed out of the church. She clutched a hymnal to her chest and as she passed Bell, who stood on the front steps, she waved goodbye. Though he was talking to his mother and another older woman, his eyes found hers and he kept her with a glance. And when he moved away from them, he said, Your playing is mighty fine, mighty fine. Everybody thinks so.

Thank you, she said and wanted to say more, something easy and generous, but was instead struck with the feeling she had whenever she was around him, that she could not find her normal speaking voice. It was not just because she was afraid he would find out she was living with Orren unmarried, but something more, some feeling that her tongue was a limp and useless thing before him. She felt herself almost shied by him. And because of this, she knew he found her nature sweeter than it was and more compliant, but as much as that was not the true state of her — her roughcut life had never afforded her the luxury of mildness — she found herself unable to change it. Or unwilling to try.

Miss Aloma, Bell said, we got a prayer meeting that gets together on Sunday afternoons that you might could be interested to attend. We'd like to see you there.

She thought about that for a second as his face was bent down earnestly toward hers so that she could see the risen color on his cheeks and even the pinhole pores there and she thought how Orren would roll his eyes at this, and that more than any real desire made her say, I don't mind to, and Bell smiled, Good. But when she was home again, she was careful not to mention it, saying merely that she was needed at the church in the late afternoon. Orren only nodded, unconcerned, and she bristled silently at this. Some part of her wanted him to mind, wanted him to say, But I don't hardly see you ever, which he might have said once, at least she imagined. Except that she couldn't know that for certain, there had not been a once upon a time in the big house, only the time before the big house when they lived apart and came together in a way that was more collision than cohabitation. Everything else was conjecture. But Aloma took Orren's indifference without comment and went back to the church in the late afternoon.

She found a small group of six, all relatively young, but still older than her, sitting on folding chairs in the space between the landing and the first pews. When she came hesitantly up the aisle, Bell sat up straight in his chair and said, Good to see you, Miss Aloma, and they turned to her, three men and two women, and she felt the faint burn of their appraisal as she approached. One of the men stood up and unfolded a chair that was leaning against the pew and he offered it to her. She took it, but set her chair just slightly out of the perfect circle of their chairs. Then Bell was speaking again as he had been before she arrived and she realized suddenly that she had not brought a Bible — not that she had one to bring — and she reached for one, stealthy as she could manage, that lay on the first pew. Bell's eyes followed her, but he didn't pause and she parted the book randomly, rested it open-faced on her lap.

It is the wait that eats at us, I think so too,

he said, picking up again after the interruption. But I believe that's what we're called to do, to keep ourselves as something precious and wait. That don't mean a prayer gets answered. We can't know the workings of God. I think we leave that to faith, he said. Leave that to faith and a good conscience, and not be like them that have put away faith and made shipwreck. It's written.

Aloma had no idea what he was talking about and she looked at the others around her and saw them nodding and she nodded too in a kind of unrealizing sympathy. One of the women saw her and smiled and then put her head down a bit, looked at her own white tennis shoes. The woman's long hair, thin at the ends, hung below the metal seat of her chair. Bell smiled at Aloma and said, We're talking about marriage.

Oh, what about it? she said, and then either because she simply realized of her own accord or she saw the halting looks on their faces, her heart sank and she saw it for the singles group that it was.

Waiting for marriage, what we do while choosing to grow in solitude, he said. That's what we're talking about.

Uh-huh, she said, yes, and she nodded and then could not help but turn and look at the front door far behind her. She longed suddenly like a house-bound dog to be on the other side of it. Then she forced herself to turn around again, blinked at her companions, and settled in to endure. Only the two women talked, the men mostly sat. Aloma sat motionless in her chair and felt the sun on her back, she flipped the frayed Bible ribbon from place to place. She herself said nothing, but watched them regain their voices once they grew accustomed to her presence. They spoke of their desire for some kind of matching that might be made for them, by God, or by chance, though they believed God. It made her think of Orren back at the farm and she wondered what he was doing while she sat here in this circle of strangers — their unselfconscious longing filling her with a deep unease, almost a spite — and where he was at this moment. She did not know, there was his innerness. It was his land, though he had said, This is ours now, that first day when she had arrived in her truck and saw the peeling house and the fields for the first time. She thought again of the day he had called her after the funeral and said, You'll come down, and she had said, Yes, yes, without hesitating. It occurred to her now that she should have paused, it would have been wise to think it over, but any hesitation would have been a lie. She did not, could not hesitate. She went down. And now, with the sun on her back and a Bible on her lap, she did not know where he was and she barely knew where she was. She remembered the way he had been when she'd first known him, when he drove her out on the veering roads and they always ended up back at the settlement school and before the night was through, her shirt was ridden up around her neck and it felt like he was trying to push his way inside her without even bothering to take off her jeans. She remembered what it was to be furiously happy like that. She drew up the two halves of the Bible and let it fall open on her lap as happenstance guided it. She read the verse before her: Better to visit the house of mourning than the house of feasting, for to be mourned is the lot of every man and the living should take this to heart. She scowled at the verse, shifted hard in her seat, and snapped the book shut. It was not like one of her scores, she could never find in it what she needed.

The hour drew on into two and more, she watched the deepening yawn of the sun verging on their little circle. Then she noticed the others begin to shift and stretch and when Bell closed his own Bible, leaning back in his seat with his hands over his belly, she darted up from her chair, mouthing to him, I've got to go, and then she left the church. She realized once she was out the door that she still had the Bible in her hands, but rather than go back in, she stowed it under her seat on the floorboard of her truck. Then she drove away.

★ ★ ★

There was no sign of Orren's truck at the farm when Aloma returned. She wandered around the left side of the house to where the fields opened up below her and stood with one hand shielding her eyes. It was breezeless. She wiped her face with the underside of her shirt, looked out over the bottomland like it was a centerless sea, her eyes settling on nothing. The tobacco plants were already showing new signs of growth after the topping, their leafy stretch widened despite the lack of rain, and they had lost the look of faded old party favors. New green shoots were ready to be suckered.

But nowhere in the midst of all those plants did she see Orren. She decided as she walked to bring in the cows herself, draw them in from the pond so that Orren would not have to do it when he returned. With the rooster killed and Orren assuring her they could do without another so long as the broody's eggs hatched, she was no longer afraid to venture near the barn and the pasture. She passed the hens all huddled in the shadows, silent and scratchless, struck dumb by the heat. She picked her way across the field, stepping high to avoid cow droppings and the pitching up and down of the natural fall of the ground. Crossing toward the pond she saw instead the cows gazing down at her stilly from the dark closeting shade on the hill and she changed direction, climbed the rise toward them. Once there, she kept going, passed from the warm sunlight into the darkness of the trees past the cows, who turned their solemn heads toward her. On into the cooler, deeper stand of trees. One cow turned slowly and followed her. The others stayed on the perimeter and watched her recede with their wide dispassionate eyes.

Aloma found to her surprise that once she passed the white oaks that lined the outer edge of the hillside, there were pines behind them. Here the needles were littered and piled so deep on the forest floor that a person could lie down and sleep on them. Orren's grandfather had not set the fence at the edge of the trees, but farther back so it extended — crooked here and there around a tree — thirty feet into the pines. The cows were free to wander back into the woods a ways, which they did during the heat of the day, reemerging toward evening to feed and water again. Aloma walked to the fence and tested it with her hands. Rusted, it streaked her palm a visceral orange. She prodded one of the barbed knots with a thumb and then carefully hoisted herself up, falling back to the ground twice before she managed to clear the fence, grasping a riven post for balance, her skirt snatched up under one arm so it would not snag. She managed to cross it uncut. She smoothed her skirt down and looked back at the cow that had followed. The cow stopped a few feet from the fence and stood gazing steadily at her with its black, mothering eyes. For a moment, Aloma did not move farther but stared back into that depth, which she found to be impossibly dark, a windowless room. Then she turned and passed twenty feet farther where the pines gave way again to white oak and peeling ash, their roots threading the ground beneath her feet. She stood in the flagging light filtered by the trees. Sweat beads cooled on her upper lip and she reached out to touch a tree beside her, and she leaned against it in relief. Her eyes closed and into the vacancy of her thoughts, Bell found his way. She blinked him away, pushed off from the tree with more force than needed, and walked on, half forgetting the cows, wondering if the woods would turn her out at the ridge road or carry her deeper. She felt she would rather stay in the woods, maybe for a long time before ever wishing to return to the house and as she turned to her left found a space that was even cooler, darker, and saw a carving on one tree. The letters *E + C* chipped into the underbelly beneath the bark. For a moment, she gazed on it in mere curiosity and nothing more, then with a start knew that it must mean Emma and Cassius, Cassius who had been the father of Cash and Orren, and she pressed one finger to her lips as if to still the woods around her and leaned in. The wood sliced for these names had darkened with age so it paled against the bark like the desiccated flesh of a yellow fruit. She ran a finger along the fretted letters, her eyebrows drew together and filled with a stern feeling, she wished suddenly that not a single one of them had ever been born to fit a blade in their hand to make vain impermanent markings on living things.

She straightened up, surprised at herself. Somewhere in the distance a door slammed, then echoed rockily against the ridge wall. She stepped suddenly away from the tree and looked around as if for someone and started back toward the house, disregarding the thickets that stabbed at the edges of her hem. The cow remained standing where she'd left her. When she crossed back over the fence and said, Get, in her voice she recognized some of the flat veneer of Orren's own voice and reached back to pat the cow on the broad, tufted sworl between her eyes, but the cow did not like this and tossed her head to one side and then walked ahead of Aloma out of the woods into the sun. Aloma shielded her eyes with her hand and followed its swinging backside as she walked slowly down the hillock to the open pasture. The other cows fell into step behind Aloma, the oldest one nearly knocking into her when she stumbled once in a snake hole. The pregnant cow came last, her gravid weight resisting each step with its sheer bulk. Across the low-chewed field, toward the red barn, into the pen, the gate of which Aloma held open for them as they passed one by one. She held the skirt of her dress up above her knees as she waited. When she came down alone around the corner of the barn, she found Orren's truck parked alongside the barn wall on the far side. With gloved hands, he grabbed bales of hay out of the bed and pitched them with a hard swinging motion against the barn in neat-enough piles to be pulleyed up to the mow. When he saw her, he said, Help me here, but then he took in her dress and he said, Oh, and waved his hand at her so she just stood beside the truck, at first leaning against it, but then not, because it was too hot, and watched him work. He moved quickly, as if any pause at all would destroy his momentum as he swung and swung and swung. It was very late in the day, the sun was shuttered by the house. She stared at Orren. The muscles under his skin were such that she had trouble taking her eyes away from them, not because they were beautiful, which they were, but because they showed her so clearly the ways in which he was not her, could not be like her. She had a sudden urge to reach out and touch the skin that held the rest of him in, but he was working and sweating so she didn't, she just watched. But she thought, Could I move like him, could my back curve and straighten like that, the ropy muscles like water that runs over rocks but not too quickly, over rocks that are smooth and not sharp. She looked at the red-brown of his darkened skin and then she looked at herself, her own pale skin. It was shocking really, she thought, what all entailed the difference between her and him, as if a whole new person could be made from the sum of that difference.

When he was done, they both climbed into

the cab of the truck and he drove it out of the field, opening the gate and then shutting it behind him, something she would have done, but he did not ask her because she was wearing a dress, and drove up along the south side of the house where he shifted into first and cut the motor.

You want something to drink? she said and he nodded, his face looked rained upon from sweat. In the kitchen she made lemonade from a mix, stirring it until the vivid yellow sediment fanned and dissolved. She poured it into a tall glass and with the glass in her hand, she went out back again and found him sitting on the lowered tailgate of his truck, his boots not touching the ground, the triangulated tips pointed down. He made sounds under his breath, inchanting so soft she almost didn't hear it, almost mistook it for breathing.

What's that you're singing? she said. She sat beside him and held the glass in her hand for a moment, the icy wet hoop ice-branding the palm of her hand.

Nothing, he said.

No, what?

He shook his head.

Tell me . . .

He turned his head fractionally away and said, with no tune, When I was sinking down, sinking down, sinking down. You know it, he said, a sideways glance to see if this was the case, his lip twisted down in apology.

Sing it, she said.

I can't sing, he said.

No, just sing it more. So he sang in a soft and artless voice, And when from death I'm free, I'll sing on, I'll sing on, and when from death I'm free, I'll sing on. The graveled pitches fought to escape his throat, but they could not rise and the unchurched sound of his voice was thin and breathed through like wind in cane.

Yes, she said and she wagged her finger before him as if she were pulling the words from his mouth with her hand.

And when from death I'm free, I'll sing and joyful be and —

He could not see that she was smiling at him because he had turned his face again into the falling sunlight on his right side, into the west.

— and through eternity, I'll sing on.

I'll sing on, she sang, her voice clear. And through eternity — but he only hummed the rest under his breath.

Yes, she said again. The sound fell away, words fallen short of their pitches, unable to form a melody, and she was left to study that side of his face. His loose curls reddened from the sun and also the granitic edge of his jaw, the hint of paler skin under his jaw and the cording of his neck. She watched the muscles in his throat work as he swallowed once. The edge of his turned face was lit then like the nimbic burning line of a cloud, so fine and bright that she turned her gaze away and saw then a flock of birds, barn swallows from the look of them but too far away to tell for sure, that had risen up in a chorus and taken to the air. They flew out together in what was a strange and shifting shape over the tobacco field, out and up, thinning for a moment so that they were no more than a blade in the sky and then swooping down now, lost in the distant shadow of the mountains. She looked at Orren again and raised her hand to point as if to say, Look what was showed us, but Orren was still turned away, the radiance of his face hidden. Aloma let her hand remain in the air for a moment and when she looked back to the birds, they were gone. She sighed, felt the unmoving weight of Orren beside her. She leaned into him just barely so their shoulders touched.

Sing it again, she said softly.

Come on, now, was his only reply, folding his cracked dry hands, one over the other between his knees, his shoulders hunched. He stayed sitting beside her looking out over the land to the west while she turned her head away with a deeper sigh and squinted into the darkening east as though searching for something. And she thought to herself with a bitterness she did not recognize because she'd not felt its tannins on her heart before, No, I will not tell him about the tree today. And maybe not any day.

★ ★ ★

After she had been playing at the church for a few weeks, Aloma felt she would be welcome to come in during the weekdays to practice piano. She wanted to leave the big house, its common graceless interior that she'd ordered but no longer wanted to master. She dreamed once or twice that it fell down while they slept and she'd woken with a start, but it was still there all around her, still strange and unchanged. She had not lost the desire to resurrect some of her better pieces to use as audition material to get into a piano program. Just as she'd always planned before she'd followed Orren. Or, if nothing else, just to hear the old music again, to remember what it was like to sit beside Mrs. Boyle with the eye of the woman on her every move, a strict attention. It had stirred her to be seen. So she decided. She abandoned the house — her cleaning, her organizing, her standing at the back door gazing dull and dry-eyed into the fields where Orren might or might not be found — and drove in to practice. The first time she went to the church it was noon. The front door was locked and dark and she stood before the peeling white doors for a few minutes like a child, her back to the road, wondering if Bell Johnson might show up. When he did not, she slouched to her truck and drove home.

She called him that night, when she was sure he would be home, and said, Do you think I might could come by the church to play tomorrow?

Well, he said, we keep it locked up during the day unless Mother's there cleaning. I run our farm during the day, mostly, but I go in generally from four to six and you're welcome to come by any time then.

The next day she pulled into the lot exactly at four and Bell Johnson did the same. He waited politely for her to get out of her truck, and when she reached for her box of scores, he took them from her. She did not protest, but followed behind him and was shied slightly by the fact that he wore jeans and an old festival tee shirt and looked younger a bit than he was.

What's all this in here? he said.

It's my scores, she said.

Sheet music.

Yeah, from when I played all the time at school.

What school was that? he said and put the box down by the piano and turned to her with his hands on his hips.

Just a settlement school east of here, she said and squatted down by the box, her face tilted slightly away to deflect further questions. She took the lid off the box and felt him towering over her, watching her.

You played all that? he said, looking over her shoulder. Mozart, huh. Alright, he said. Well. He took a step away from the piano. I got a little office off the kitchen. If you need a thing, don't hesitate.

For a moment more, he did not move. She smiled up at him — just for a second — and he, feeling that the conversation could not go further, but not knowing why, left. Then she pulled the first score from the box and spread it on the rack of the piano, her heart beating. She looked up at the door Bell had closed behind him. She hesitated, her hands hovering above the keys. Then she played. And she played, not with the smoothness that she'd possessed two months ago — the last time she'd played from any of the scores

— but with a surging and unsteady need that had not been there before. As her fingers found their home, clumsy at first but quick to confidence, her body rocked back and forth unaware on the bench like a child finding its comfort. She played and played.

So she came four times a week to practice, not including Wednesday, and she practiced the old music, the Grieg and Schumann, the Bach she played badly but loved, Beethoven and Liszt, and she thought how much she had missed all this. And she thought too how Orren did not know this part of her, he'd not once seen her play piano, she believed he didn't know what she was capable of. Who she could be.

Bell met her every day at the front door. He learned quickly that she would always come on time so he was sure never to be late and he waited on the front steps until she turned into the lot and then he stood and tossed his keys lightly in his hand. Once her pattern was established, it was always like this and he was always there. But once he let her into the building and was polite — he was always polite, but nothing more — he disappeared into the back and she played until six when she left without seeing him again. He stayed in his office and she knew he heard her, because her playing crashed through the small sanctuary and the walls were paper-thin. After a week and a half of this, she was restless. So one day, not thinking it unwise, not really thinking anything about it at all, she went to the office and peeked her head around the door, saw him sitting at a desk with his Bible spread open before him, a pen lolled between two thickly made fingers. She said, So this is where you work. She had caught him by surprise and he looked up, startled. Then he sat back on his chair and brought his hands together, clasping the pen over his belly. He smiled, looking up at her face tilting forward and gleaming from the door frame that she gripped. Expectation perched in the set of her lips.

This is it, he said slowly. It ain't much.

Well, I don't have an office. I think it's pretty nice.

He looked at her and measured her words for a moment before he said, So I reckon you're no secretary if you don't have a office.

No, she said.

What's it you do exactly?

Well, this mostly, she said. She picked at nothing on the grain of the wood.

He cocked his head to the side, still smiling. That don't add up, he said. How do you eat?

Well, I've got a little money saved up, she

said, which was true. She had exactly sixty dollars saved, which amounted to all the money she had made in one month at the job.

He nodded as if he understood. She turned abruptly and faced the door frame then, tapped her nails against the wood in a confounded rhythm, smiled as if she might laugh and then stopped herself. Looked at him again, looked away, and said, I guess I ought to play some more.

I reckon, he said. And she left. But the next day, after she had been playing for about an hour, he wandered out to the sanctuary, or at least to the door, and stood there and listened as she played and she knew he was there but pretended she didn't. The next day he came all the way in. He stood by the piano for a moment and then went to the landing and sat down behind the piano a ways so that she could not see him, except for the length of his legs from the knees down. When she finished, she put her hands in her lap and leaned over to peer at him.

That's some good playing, he said and he was shaking his head. How long you played like that?

Oh, eight or nine years, she said. I learned this piece when I was fifteen.

What is it? he said.

It's a wedding march, but not the one you

always hear, the one they always play. This is one people don't ever get married to.

No kidding, he said and he laughed. Well, how would I know, I ain't never been married.

I gathered that.

And now maybe I'm too old, he said and he looked over at her.

No, she said.

Thirty-six, he said. I'm a old man now. He smiled, watching.

That's not really old, she said, but her denial seemed to confirm something for him and he looked out at the empty pews. They were silent.

You never did come back to the singles meeting, he said suddenly.

Oh, that, she said with a wave of her hand. That cut into my alone time.

He laughed, really laughed, with his head tossed back and she was pleased with herself and played a few trivial notes on the keyboard. When he quieted, he jointed his hands before him, his elbows on the white worn knees of his jeans. No, he said, I never married. Honestly, I don't think folks care for it that much. But my daddy preached this church and that's how I came to be here. They tolerate it, I suspect. I do the best I can for them.

Oh, I don't think they tolerate you. They think you're good at what you do.

Thank you, he said. I suspect they'd all just feel better if I had a wife.

Well, how come you never got married?

He looked intent on the pews. I guess I just never found that special girl.

Special girl, huh, Aloma said, raising her arched hands to the keys again and finding a few more notes, but still leaning to watch him. Why does she have to be so special? Is that because you think you're so special?

She'd meant it as a joke, but he didn't smile. His gaze faltered down and he moved his mouth as if he chewed on something sour, the muscle there belled and sank once. His color rose. Aloma righted quickly in her seat and began to play to cover her own embarrassment. With nothing in mind, she invented on the keys until she settled into G and without really choosing it, she began to play the hymn Orren had been humming the day she brought in the cows. She had not seen the hymn in a long time, but her fingers found the progressions and she closed her eyes and the bars came before her eyes like a scroll.

When the last chord rang out into the silent sanctuary, she opened her eyes and braved a glance at Bell and his face was turned down now, his thumbs pressed like stoppers to the inner corners of his eyes. When he looked up, awoken from himself, she saw the wetness on his cheeks. Aloma shrank behind the piano wall, sat there hunched in her ill ease, unable to reconcile herself to the tenderheartedness of mountain boys, not knowing whether to say something, say nothing, or play. She waited. But when he said nothing, nor moved one inch, and the silence had grown too large for the room, she said, I'm sorry. She did not know what she was sorry for.

No, no, he said, sounding very formal suddenly, his voice thick as if he were speaking through a mouth full of cotton wool.

She peered around the piano again. Did I do something wrong? she said, her hands sliding the dust from the slip below the keys where he could not see them.

He stretched his neck, first to the right, then to the left as though it hurt. That's a hymn we sang at Daddy's funeral. He looked at her with a funny little grin. He wanted that one, he said. It was his favorite. I can't have thought of it in quite a while. You took me by surprise. Ain't that funny, he said, more to himself than to her. Funny how somebody can pass and be gone a long time and then something . . . happens, you hear a snatch of music and it feels all over again like they can't be dead. Like their dying was just a mean trick of memory or something like that. But they are really gone from this place, I guess. There's a resurrection, there's a time for reuniting. That's what that feeling is, I guess, knowing it beforehand, disbelieving they're dead. Your head says they're dead, but then you feel that they can't be dead, not really, and it's the feeling that's the knowing. I do believe that. He surveyed the small sanctuary. Then he cleared his throat and looked at her and his eyes were very open. Course, you're very young. I reckon you still got your folks.

No, they're dead.

He started back. Oh, forgive me. I ought not to a said that.

She shrugged. They've been dead since I was three. I don't remember anything. And it was true. She didn't remember a kiss or a scent or even any sentiment other than a muted awareness that they were gone to associate with them. As a child, she'd tried to invent the feeling of loss inside her. But like the dead, the feeling simply wasn't there. It was not that her uncle and aunt filled up the space that her parents vacated; it was just that the empty space was fine as it was and no more hurtful than being born with four fingers on one hand instead of five. It was just a lack she thought didn't mean anything.

I'm very sorry, Miss Aloma, he said and he looked at her in a steady way with his surprised, almost black eyes and she tossed off, It doesn't bother me one bit, but in such a blithe manner that it sounded almost cruel — she felt it as soon as she said it — though she couldn't be sure if it was cruel to Bell, or her dead parents, or only to herself. But she'd balked at his words and the gravity of his look and she had the sour feeling that he was apprehending a grief that wasn't there. He straightened up from the steps then, sharp and a bit too fast, and he stood stiff so he looked to her eyes like a boy playing soldier. But a very tall one.

Thank you for playing that song, Miss Aloma, he said very carefully, passing a hand down the front of his shirt. Thank you very much. And he turned and passed through the door that led into the back of the building and she was left alone sitting at the piano. She watched the afternoon sun creep across the floor, slow as glass it moved before her eyes. She took up her scores in her arms then. But she laid them down again beside her on the bench, still not taking her gaze from the canted light, and placed her fingers blindly on the keys and she played. Once again, she felt the upswell of pleasure she'd been missing for so long and then a thought crossed her mind, that the preacher might be standing on the other side of the door, that he might be listening, and this gave her a different kind of pleasure, one that was new to her.

★ ★ ★

She stayed in Hansonville to shop for groceries and when she returned to the house, Orren was standing on the porch. She parked and eyed him as she climbed out of the truck, carrying a brown paper bag, and stopped before him, her feet on the slender skirting of grass. His face was so dark with sun that he did not look the same race as her.

Hello, Orren, she said and as soon as it came out of her mouth, she thought how odd it was, how cold it could sound to call a man by his given name like that. He did not seem to notice.

It's tricky, he said, not looking at her. He bit his lip and she waited for him to continue, unsure if he would. But he said, It's hell to tell a ready leaf from just a stressed leaf. He looked plainly at her then, as though waiting for something, and when she said nothing in response, he pulled up his cotton shirt from his waistband and wiped his face with it, letting it fall over his belly again striped with bands of sweat and said, From the drought. The butts look yellow, but it ain't ready. It's hard as hell to tell.

Well, can you cut them now and dry them longer?

He did not answer. Instead, he said, You been gone a whole lot.

She hauled the groceries higher on her hip. Only two hours a day.

That's how I said.

If that's a lot, you're crazy, she said and she stepped up onto the porch intending to pass him, but he held out his hand to the side so that he touched her with a single finger, his index finger, very gently, and it stayed her.

And what's it you do for two hours like that?

She stopped. I'm playing the piano, Orren. God bless.

That's all, he said.

Her eyes narrowed. Damn, Orren, she said.

Why are you calling me like that?

Cause it's your name, she said and she scathed him with her eyes top to toe. And sometimes I have to remind myself just who on earth you are. She didn't blink when she spoke, but leveled his stare with hers.

What's that supposed to mean?

It means I don't ever see you no matter that I live with you and then when I do see you, you don't have anything to say.

Aloma, listen, he said.

Oh, God forbid somebody tells you what to do, she snapped.

You ain't my mother.

She blinked, her lips parted. No, she said and lower, No, I'm not. And to that he had no response. He just cut his eyes away and in the same instant pulled his hand back to his own person, and folded his arms on his chest, looking away so she could not see his face. She shifted the weight of the bag from one hip to the other like it was a baby and she looked where he looked, out over the front acres dropping away to the trees where she had first seen his truck glinting. Then she turned her back and continued on into the house, letting the screen door slam behind her.

*   *   *

She woke up in the middle of the night and her first thought was that it was cool out of season and that was a relief. She stretched her limbs, but then she realized that the sheets were pushed away from her shoulders and chest and the bed was empty. Aloma started in the bed and looked around her at the darkened room. Orren stood by the window, the moonlight glazing white on the black and blue of his shadowed skin. For a moment she only stared at him, they had not spoken more than mere necessities after their words on the front porch. She thought now about saying nothing out of remnant spite and pretending to still be asleep, but when he did not move and did not even look to be breathing — his chest was still as if he were made of wood — she spoke.

What are you looking at?

He did not seem surprised when her voice broke the stillness of the room, he did not change position and he took his time answering. I don't know, he said.

You must be looking at something.

He glanced over his shoulder at her and the moonlight lit the left side of his face, cast the right side into strange deep shadow so that he appeared suddenly to have only one eye. She looked away from that, worked out the wrinkles on the sheet beside her with her finger.

Tell me, she said, her eyes cast down.

I can't see nothing really, he said, turning back around and looking up through the glass. The moon keeps coming and going.

Yeah, she said, sifting through his tone for the tiniest apology.

Then he said, I ever tell you I been down to

Mammoth Cave once?

No. She looked up, surprised, and sat up higher on her old feather pillow.

Before Daddy died, he said, we gone down. Before he died . . . It was a vacation or something. We drove down there. And we was in this cave and the tour fellow turned off the flashlight. Orren turned now with his whole body, turned fully into his own shadow so she saw him only as a silhouette and she sensed that his whole body was watching her like a watchful face.

And what happened? she said.

Nothing, he said. It just was dark. But it was dark like you ain't never seen dark before, like you can't see your hand in front of your own face and I couldn't tell where nobody was and you don't know if there's a up or down or not. That's how dark. Not like this dark here — he nodded back out the window toward the grass beyond the windowpane — where you can still see something. It made everything just gone, he said. Then he folded his arms over his chest and said, And then when that flashlight come on, everybody in there just laughed. Even my folks. He stopped suddenly and peered out the window as though his eye had found something there.

They were relieved probably, Aloma said.

Well, he said, I ain't liked it, I never could reconcile to it. It was like people laughing at a dead dog on the side of the road. Something that just ain't funny.

She had no response to that. When he spoke again, he said softer, It better rain.

It's gonna rain, Orren, she said, petting him this time with his name when she spoke it. I won't let it not.

He snorted and looked out the window again. Well, it best, he said, cause this place is riding to hell quicker than ... And he struggled for the rest of the sentence, Aloma saw his lips working for a moment more, but his sentence died.

Aloma stretched again, pushed the rest of the tangled sheets away from the twin converging lines of her bare legs. Orren, she said. He took his time turning around again, but then he only stood there reluctant and the moonlight figured around him and the front of him was altogether dark again so she could not see his expression. She laid her hands on her breasts and felt the dilute blue wash of light on her own face. A strange sensation passed over her as Orren walked slowly around the bed to his side and sat down, placing one hand flat against the headboard. My granddaddy built this bed, he said. He built it in the curing barn. Aloma waited for more and then pulled at his elbow with one hand until he turned around and lay down beside her. I wish you'd tell me more things, she said and they kissed and then neither she nor he said anything further. He moved slowly over her, he settled between her legs, and she said his name again, but all the while she was watching his shadow-strange face in the dark, she felt a small dawning fear. She felt she did not know this face, this stranger, not at all, but also she did not care then, stranger or not, as she gripped hard the top rear of his thigh and pressed him into her. His face gasped once for air. Then she was pulling him into his motions and holding him against her. But even as she grasped at him ever tighter with her hands, allowing him no distance at all from her chest, she sensed that she was merely knocking at the door of his flesh, and that even when he cried out and she felt him give up to her, the door did not open.

★   ★   ★

Aloma was restless and unable to account for it. She'd drifted anchorless through the house all day swiping at random surfaces with a polishing rag, talking to herself, standing glassy-eyed before the portraits until her own thoughts fell away and she forgot herself and she remembered Orren's nightwatch at the window. Then, against her will, even as she blamed him for her restlessness, she felt a creeping reluctant desire for the very things he wanted, something for the land itself and the tobacco that meagered its little water from the soil. She found that if she fastened her eyes to the ground at her feet where she could not see the wave of earth beyond the fields, she could hold on to the feeling. So long as she did not look up.

When Orren came up the hill in the late afternoon, the fish and greens were glazed and cooling and Aloma stood waiting for him in the kitchen. He came, holding himself upright by what appeared only a faltering act of will, for two times he stopped as though he had forgotten something and turned around to peer back behind him — at what, Aloma did not know. When he turned back again and came on, he looked drawn as if the daylight that sapped the soil sapped some essential in him as well. Aloma opened the door for him and trailed after him into the dining room, noting the lifeless hang of his hands at his sides and the tired rise of one shoulder, higher than the other, as if it alone could not accept defeat. When he sat back in his chair reaching for his cigarettes, which

158

Aloma snatched off the table because she could not tolerate him to smoke in the house, she said, You do too much.

I do a lot, he conceded. But no need to hire nobody and no money to do it. I got some things to figure out. I just got to get through this season. He pointed at the paperwork at the other end of the table.

Well, I was thinking, Aloma said, I could do more around here, you know. A girl can do more.

I know it, said Orren. Mama done everything. We was just boys when Daddy died. She done it all, she made it run.

Oh, said Aloma, vaguely disappointed by this answer. She looked down at her plate. Well, you might could give the barn over to me. I'll get the eggs and stuff and feed the chickens.

Now that the rooster's gone.

She looked up again, narrowed her eyes. Well.

He pondered it for a second and scratched at one reddish sideburn as though it itched. Well, yeah, he said. If you want to. You might could take the chickens. And feed them. Put not too much oyster in it, though. And I want you to stay away from that broody.

She shrugged thinly.

He eyeballed her. You ever done it? he said.

159

Done what . . .

Took care of chickens.

What do you think? she said, too sharp. Her cheeks stained with a flush that he saw, he saw as he watched her face. She crossed her arms over her breasts and drew one lip under the line of her teeth. It wasn't her fault she'd been born into a doublewide of nothing and then spent the better part of her childhood in a school at the sink end of a holler. She'd learned piano. It was something he could never have.

Well, don't be hateful, he said. Nobody said you can't do it. I'm only asking.

Well, so learn me it, she said, cocking her head, and he seemed not to catch the hint of mock in her voice.

He walked with her down to the barn and as they approached, the calico cats scattered.

What are the names of those cats? Aloma said.

If they had ones, nobody told it to me. He paused for a moment, watching them flee, and then he walked ahead of her into the dark interior where it smelled like hay and old wood and chicken shit sharpened and made acrid by the heat of the day. The sun, in short shafts, angered the old boards. Light slanted thick and yellow and everything it touched in the barn — the now-empty horse stalls, the bent and broken hay scattered, the backs of their own legs — was heated by it. Orren stood beside her and surveyed the barn interior for a brief moment before he spoke.

That's the broody and you don't mess with her, he said. He pointed to a hen he'd situated in her own coop, set apart from the others that stuttered fat and gawky on their yellow root-twist legs, not confined to coops or the boxes on the laying wall. The broody sat russet behind her chicken wire and looked to be asleep or near death from boredom. If we get up those chicks, then we might could do without a rooster a while longer, Orren said. He gave Aloma a look that she refused to acknowledge, looking elsewhere around the barn but listening hard nonetheless. We got plenty of hens and just for laying. So we can do without for a bit. So just leave her be and I'll feed her so if she's jumpy, she's remembered of me. I just don't want to lose those chicks.

Okay, she said.

Here's the feed. He reached her the chaff-dusted sack in the corner of an unused stall. Now use about this much and add about this much oyster shell and fill up the trough and then you just scatter it like so, and he scattered it so it fell onto the barn floor near the laying wall, but not before it caught the setting light and shone like brief gold as it fell. Some of the chickens came and pecked. Two ran into each other.

My God, these chickens are stupid, Aloma said.

Yeah, well, he said, nodding, and when he looked at her, she saw in the light very clearly again the increase of age around his eyes, age that had come quick. He dusted his hands off on his jeans and then placed one hand on her shoulder and she felt suddenly that she was his young daughter and not his should-be wife, or his girlfriend, or whatever she was here in this place, his grandfather's barn.

Mama didn't know none of it when Daddy died, he said. She just learned it. Then he stepped away from her and made to leave the barn, but stopped instead with his back to her. He gripped the frame of the wide door with his left hand, his fingers brailled the wood for a moment.

Aloma eyed him as the chickens scratched around her, their bobbing bodies polka-dotted with white like bleach spots, and she stepped through them, paddling the air with both hands to shoo them so that they parted like a bobbing stream. She reached for the cribbed top of a stall door and it gave slightly under her hand, swinging into the interior so that she stumbled forward a bit into the palfried air. She stood with one foot in the stall, one out. Against one wall, a half-rotted bridle hung, the cheekpiece torn, its leather pilled with age. Old orange saddle pads lay stacked on the hay in the stall. She imagined they still held the heat of a horse like a sheet come out of a dryer.

I bet you miss the horses sometimes, huh, she said to Orren's back.

No, he said. Just another body I can't afford to feed.

I'd miss a horse if I had one.

Goddamn.

What? she said. She let go the gnawn wood.

How can it be so goddamn humid and so goddamn dry, he said questionless out to the day and he held one hand out like an empty dipper.

I don't know, Orren, she said, stepping out of the stall, moving toward him. But it'll rain. You just gotta have faith.

He turned then, turned to look at her, and as he did, the small black pupil of his eye expanded suddenly, she saw it grow as he turned away from the light toward the pitching shadows of the barn where she stood, erupting blackly against the thinning blue of his eye. How come's that, Aloma? he said.

163

She stopped before him. Because things work out, she said slowly, considering his wide black pupils.

Is that right? he said.

Well, yeah, she said.

He opened his mouth to say something, but then closed it again. The corner of his lip tucked in.

What? she said.

He shook his head as though he were about to turn and leave, but instead he reached out with his hand and took her face. He drew her close. With his thumb against the dimple of her chin, he turned her face first to the left, then to the right as if seeing the architecture of her face for the first time, studying on the prospect of shelter to be found there.

What? she said again, about to pull away.

Mama used to say silly shit like that.

It's not silly, she said, bristling and straightening away from him. But he followed her, he stepped in, the enormous black of his pupils sweeping by her line of vision as he lowered his head and kissed her once on the spot on her chin where his thumb had been.

It's worse than silly, he said when he straightened up.

She pulled away in earnest then, accidentally bumping a hen that pecked too close to her heels. She scowled down at it once, but said nothing further.

I know you mean good, Orren said as he himself moved away, turning from her to face his withered fields. Most of the time, he tossed over his shoulder, stepping out of the barn.

★　★　★

On the steps of the church on Sunday morning, Bell greeted as he always did, but when it came time for the service to begin, he walked to the front of the church and sat in the front row before the lectern. He leaned his head down, resting it on one hand, his fingers splayed across his temple and hairline so Aloma could not see his face from where she sat. An old man rose from a front pew in his stead. He rolled an easy, familiar patter of prayer and supplication, but there were no calls from the pews. Those gathered were distracted and they watched Bell, or at least the curve of his long back as he sat before them, with them. In the silence following his prayer, the old man moved slowly back to his seat. When he did, Bell sat up straight, and appearing to stretch as he extended himself to his full height, he stood. He did not carry a Bible up the three steps and when he stood behind the lectern, he remained there only long enough to draw a breath before he abandoned it and returned to the first step of the landing. He raised his eyes, they had been cast down.

I'm not fixing to preach on something other than what's troubling our minds, so I got to preach on rain, have to preach on rain, he said and he sounded as if he were speaking in a much smaller room than the one that held them all, his voice was so low. But I ain't got a lot to say on it, all I got is prayers. So maybe today this is less a sermon and more a prayer group, because we need the rain, brothers and sisters, we need rain. Most of us got a harvest that's got to come, because that's how we're fed, it's our bread and butter. And it's not coming and we're wondering why and what we've done and what we can do.

Bell paused and gazed out over them and Aloma felt that his eyes found all of them, though this could not be so, as he was only one man and there were so many of them. He did not smile when he looked over them, his mouth was a line.

I can't read you the meaning of this dry spell, he said. I suspect there's no kind of meaning at all. I got to be honest, he said, I don't see God's hand in everything. Well, I do and I don't, it's hard to reckon. Maybe his hand is on everything, but maybe it ain't in everything, the Scripture gives it to us both ways, so I don't know, I don't know. For who is like the wise man and knoweth the interpretation of a thing. That's written, that's written. I can't read the meaning. Maybe it's a test, but I don't know I believe in tests. I know some of you do, but I don't. Maybe we can work that out later when we're pearls in heaven, I don't know. I don't suspect God is tricky like that, but I can't say for sure. Can you? And that leads me to despair. He rested his hands on his hips and looked out into the faces that waited, some that were lifted up and some that were tilted toward the floor, and he stepped forward off the last step so that he stood at the first pew's knees.

And I know you are despairing too, he said and grinned with a sad corner of his mouth. What looks like patience tastes like despair. I feel it and I know it not just in my mind but in my heart too. God laid despair on my heart and it learns me yours, he said, and he placed his palm flat over his heart. And the thing is, the dust bowl wasn't so long ago now, was it, Mother's and your all's folks lived through that, some of you too. It was bad enough here with the burley, but it was worse out West. The rivers dried up and the animals died. And when those people saw it happen, they despaired — and I believe we would too — and they said to themselves, the fate of the animals and the fate of the humans is the same; as one dieth, so dieth the other. They all take up the same breath and humans got no rightful advantage over the animals, and listen to me, I am not blaspheming, brothers and sisters, it's written: who knoweth whether the human spirit goeth upward and the spirit of the animals goeth downward? That's what they asked. It's written and it's despair that wrote it and God forgives it or he wouldn't a let it to lie here — and he lifted the Bible right off the lap of the woman before him and held it up so its gold lettering flicked in the light. He said, He forgives despair. God says it's alright to grieve and wonder, brothers and sisters, and we do. We grieve and wonder how come the rain won't fall and we know there's a answer to that despair, because that despair is a question, it ain't a answer, that's what we got to remember: God is the answer, the four gospels is a answer to that despair and to where our spirits go. And yet — he paused, breathed, and said — man will be to suffer. And his voice fell to nothing for a moment as he ruminated and placed one hand in his pocket, and then removed it and shook it against his thigh as if he were rattling a tambourine against his thigh. He looked up and smiled. He gripped the Bible tighter. He waited a moment, just smiling, and then he said, But, hallelujah, it's going to rain. He handed the Bible back to the woman in the first pew and the amens thundered out and he let them fall before continuing, It is going to rain. It is going to rain and God says so and I'm only preaching it to you now because he invested me with the body to say it to you today. Brothers and sisters, the upright abideth in the land, it's written. It is going to rain, but I'm not telling God that, God's telling me that. I'm not demanding — but then Bell's voice rose and he demanded — but it will rain. That ain't arrogance. It's just if there's one thing I know, it's that the land is going to last. Not me, not you. We are the spirits that ascend. But the Word cannot ascend, because the Word always was. No, I promise you here it's going to rain, and the reason I know it is because the land is His, the land is God's, the land is God's own declamation, he said. The land is God's . . . He did not finish his sentence but closed his eyes and let his voice drift and they waited and when he did not open his eyes and began rather to pray in the same deep bell tone that he ended, they bowed their heads and prayed with him. And even the children who had remained up front looking around and swatting one another regardless of the drought that blew hot and dry on their parents and their homes, they also bowed their heads and quieted themselves and prayed.

★ ★ ★

In the parking lot, under the sun, they did not leave. They stood sweating and swatting at the flies, yet not a single car drove off, and it seemed that when Bell turned away from one eager face there were ten more waiting and they all wanted to speak to him — about what it didn't matter — because at home were only their farms and themselves. So they stood in slowly milling circles that opened and closed but did not disperse and they watched Bell. Aloma too could not face the thought of returning alone to the house and she sat instead on a bench just beyond the people, half turned toward her truck as if thinking of something far away but listening close to the Sunday clamor. After fifteen minutes, Bell climbed the three church steps, raised his hands, and in a loud voice said, Well, since nobody's making to leave, let's have a impromptu picnic down at the ball-park on Estill. How about in two hours, at two-thirty, everybody just bring something to eat down there. Does that give the ladies enough time — he looked down at his mother beside him and she nodded and he nodded too, looking into her eyes, and continuing, Alright, alright, and he clapped his hands twice like a bandleader. And those were the words that delivered them. In twos and threes they drove off, all of them and without delaying further, though Aloma sat where she was for a few minutes and watched them go, and watched Bell.

★ ★ ★

It took her less than forty-five minutes to make chicken in broccoli and cheese — a small miracle, as she'd learned only a month prior that chicken could be baked in the oven like a pie and not just fried to a crisp in a skillet. She slapped two sandwiches together for Orren as he watched her balefully, his shirt unbuttoned and stripped off his upper half, but hanging still from the waistband of his jeans as though he'd raptured out of it. She spread mayonnaise and bologna on bread as the chicken baked. He leaned against the counter as she paid him no mind.

What's that you're making? he said.

Sandwiches for you. What's it look like, she said without looking up.

No, that, he said, indicating with one mud-brown hand toward the oven. Kinda hot for baking, he said.

It's for church, she said.

What, you're fixing to go back? He looked up at the clock on the kitchen wall between the two large windows on the northern wall. It was almost two.

Yeah, she said. There's a picnic.

God bless, he said. Ain't they got shit to do? It's a drought.

Well, it's too dry to do much, isn't it?

Hell, he said, they can spit on their plants. Or cut their wrists. She shot him a dark look when she handed him the sandwiches stacked, but he took them and began to move off without further comment. But then he said, Next time be Christian with the bologna, and he passed out of the house and in her mind's eye he was shaking his head, though she did not glance behind her until the door slammed. Aloma stepped across the room to snatch open the door again. She watched as Orren ate the sandwiches in three bites each and walked back down toward the tobacco, struggling one arm and then the next into his shirt as he went. Aloma rested a box fan on a chair in front of the door then and sat in the breeze with her legs spread and her skirt hiked up on her thighs. The oven's heat pressed her like a hand from behind. The only sound she heard over the fan was the occasional report of wood cuffing wood, though from what direction it was coming she was unable to tell. She counted the knocking echoes as they broke.

She drove through the sweltering late afternoon trying to remember the directions to the ballpark, but it was not so clear in her mind and she took four wrong turns that led her in a loop all the way to the other side of the county before curving back around. The chicken sat under foil on the seat beside her, barely cooling. She sweated so that the back of her shirt was wet and she sat up and hugged the wheel to feel the cool breeze as it shook her shirt. Her stomach suffered. She had not eaten anything and an emptiness hovered just under her heart, a vague discomfort at the center of her. She looked repeatedly at her watch as the hour approached and passed two-thirty and that only made the feeling worse so she breathed, deep to settle herself and did that over and over until she finally turned onto the correct stretch of road and could see the ballpark with its silt-dust diamond infields in the distance. But then as she was approaching the entrance to the park — and even lifting her foot off the gas to brake — and she could make out the familiar bearing of the people from the church and Bell's figure among them, because he stood a full head over all the others, she turned her head away as though resolute on some other purpose and pressed her foot to the gas and drove straight on. She blinked, but did not turn her head to the left or the right, only lifted her left arm to rest it on the window to shield her face. She held her breath. Then she passed quickly, and once she rounded the bend at the far end of the road, she leaped the gas so that her tires spun out and left abrupt side-swiping marks on the asphalt where the road entered a line of trees. She looked at herself in her rearview and her face was wide-eyed but otherwise innocent of expression. Then she tilted the mirror toward the ceiling with her shifting hand. The foil on the chicken rattled in the wind as she sped; Orren would eat it after all. And if he asked why she brought it back, she would tell him the truth, that she had felt mysterious and ill of a sudden and could simply go no farther.

This time she took the wrong roads intentionally so that she drove the long way back to the farm. She switched the radio on, she switched it off. And as she passed out of the trees, the road rippled in the heat and she dropped her hand out the window, grabbing distractedly at woolen handfuls of air. She passed a stretch of road where the trees fell away on both sides and the mountains were just a blued thinspun haze to the east and there were open fields to the left and to the right of her. Her eyes were tired to see the tobacco sucking at the milkless soil, but there was nothing else to see, there were no houses here, not even barns. These were bigger farms than theirs, bigger than what Emma and Orren's father had farmed. And she thought to herself suddenly, Was it just like this empty stretch of road where Emma and Cash . . . She realized that she did not even know where it was that they had died, only that it was not far from the farm, somewhere near the top of the county. And she thought of Orren and how he drove off in his truck at least once a day to fetch something from the grocery or all the way in Hansonville and did he pass that spot and what must he think when he saw it . . . She thought this all for the first time. And it occurred to her then that he was the last one, he was the distillation of what had once been the complex and dilute lifeblood of a family. He was a family cut down to one. She too was a last one, but she'd never thought of herself that way, she'd never thought of it much at all. Aloma had learned of loss only by hearing that it had once happened to her, but Orren had lived that heavy change in the undying instant when the steel rumpled like hard cloth and the sheet metal sheered off in a clean slide toward the perfect brilliant glass of the windshield. And now Orren was like a man who had not heard the thing was finished, begun but not yet ended, no final word yet from that empty road. Aloma let her foot unthinkingly off the gas so that the truck slowed and nearly stopped before she realized what she had done. She blinked. She woke to her surroundings. The dust breathed up off the soil on the sides of the road and whispered out onto the blacktop, swirling into tiny eddies which the wind moved, but barely. She spied a tree that had begun to turn early in defeat. Her eyes were wide to the miscarriage of the summer, the ruth and pity of it. She suddenly desired the betterment of everything, for herself and Orren and every single thing that had ever died, or would. And for a moment, just this once, she wanted to be at the house. She pushed her truck too hard into third and the engine labored as she pressed her foot unforgivingly to the gas and drove home as if she could not get there fast enough, as if there it would not be dry.

★　★　★

The week passed and Aloma grew so wearied from waiting, she felt no relief at all when the first black cloud engulfed the northwestern horizon. She did not even notice it at first, standing as she was over the stove, her back to the world and her head down. She did not feel the air charge, abrading against itself, and did not know the winds rose up in a quarrel with the stillness. She started only when she heard Orren's voice behind her. He appeared suddenly, balanced on the threshold, gripping the old wood and leaning back, silhouetted by the bright blue stormless sky.

Aloma, he said. She wiped her hands on the sides of her blouse and followed him when he jumped off the concrete steps and disappeared around the side of the house. She found him standing on the lawn with his eyes cast up and the crown of his head tilted back. She reached out to touch the worn walls to steady herself, beyond him she saw the skeining clouds that took the horizon, the great massing bulk of the storm that had grown in silence for the better part of an hour.

Look, he said and pointed as if she had not spotted it with her own eyes. They stood and gazed on it and even as they stood with their small faces upturned, the first pass of wind came and the heat was sluiced by a new cool.

What if it changes up and fairs off? Orren said, half turning toward her with his hands on his hips, but she only shrugged, because it was not a question, not really, just hope afraid to hope.

Come eat now, Aloma said, cowed slightly before the raging horizon and already retracing her steps into the kitchen, looking over her shoulder once or twice at the rising weather.

I can't eat no food right now, Orren called after her, but by the time she was in the dining room and seated at the table, he had trailed reluctantly after her, stopping to look through each window as he passed.

Neither of them spoke while Aloma ate her own macaroni and salad, but true to his word, Orren could not eat, but only gripped his fork in his hand and passed his feet here and there under his chair like a restive horse, the heels of his boots pattered against the wood. Aloma closed her eyes as she chewed and tried her best to ignore him, but still she saw the blacker shadows of his movements against her eyelids. She opened her eyes again and watched him reluctantly, the way he tucked his head down to gaze up through the dining room window to find the blackening sky beyond the compass of their small room. His mouth was moving just barely, she could

178

not make out any words.

Suddenly thunder bucked across the width of the sky.

Holy shit, said Orren and stood up so fast that his chair scraped and upended with a clatter behind him. He left it where it toppled and stalked to the kitchen door and then back again as fast, grabbing Aloma by her elbow to pull her up from the table and then by the hand out the door into the unnatural dark of the encroaching storm. Hard, bulleting raindrops were just beginning to fall. No, she said, pulling back. With her hand still in his, he charged down past the willow, its long fronds streamed away from the white house. Aloma skipped and stumbled behind to keep up with Orren's stride. She tried to pull back her hand half from irritation and half from pain, but he held her firm, and when thunder cracked again right over their heads, she yelped and was glad he was holding her hand tight enough to hurt. Down across the wetting grass and in between the rows of tobacco, the soil ashen beneath their feet, but pockmarked now by raindrops that grayed the farm as they fell.

She's gonna break, Orren said and let go her small hand.

Orren, she said as he moved away, come back to the house before we get struck by lightning. He didn't seem to have heard, but turned and turned, trying to see the whole of the farm at once, his face unbrooding itself as he watched, turning.

Then the first full sheet of rain fell and Aloma was caught by the sudden wind that whipped her hair and her blouse, which in another instant was saturated through with rainwater so that she felt the cold on her breasts and belly.

Orren stepped out farther into the field.

Thank you, he said upward as if in prayer and brought his fisted hands together and up to his forehead and closed his eyes. His face was light with relief. The rain washed his forehead and his hands, his lips parted. Aloma held a forearm up over her eyes to shield them from the driving rain, but did not smile and she discovered no thanks in her. She could only watch the unclosing of Orren's face, which the sky had seduced from him as all around them the fulling rain beat an unsteady battering rhythm on the plants and the parched, loamy soil. Aloma retreated a few steps back toward the house with her eyes on Orren, and then with a sullenness that surprised her and that she did not foresee, she kicked out at a plant as she turned, cutting into the vibrant pith of the stalk near the soil. It did not fall, but the cut was deep. Its fluorescent green living inside was revealed. She cast a fearing glance over her shoulder, but Orren was still as she had left him, his hands before his face. Beyond him, the mountains were already enshrouded in the storm's leaden clouds so that the ridge blended into the haze and the effect was one of borderless darkness.

★ ★ ★

When Orren finally came into the house — and when he did, he ran headlong into the wind and rain that cavalried down toward the foothills where it rose and then dissipated over the coal counties — he was soaked through his clothes. Aloma made him strip down out of his jeans and his button-up shirt in the kitchen and tried to help him, peeling off the wet fabric that leeched to his skin until he stood in nothing but his white underpants and his goose-bumped flesh. But even stripped naked he could not keep to one spot but passed from window to window gripping the white flaking sills and looking up and out at the whipping slate sky and he shook his head in wonderment. Shit, he said over and over as he watched and it was with gratitude and some sense of luck shared down the ridgeline.

The Friday of the first rains turned over to Saturday and the rains kept on. The sky swelled with flumes of black, the underbellies of great waves churning that rolled continually out of the northwest and broke against the farm. The thunder came so fast and hard, Aloma walked around the house with her head ducked and her hands at the ready by her ears. At its worst, it sounded like God ripping old-growth trees out of the earth by their roots and then whipping the earth with their length so that the crack of their breaking limbs reported across the land over and over, the reverberations shuddered from one horizon to the other. Once a rage of clouds passed over, the next came rolling in so there was no rest for their nerves, and no sun. Light straked the sky in candent broken lines for hours on end, sometimes so bright at night and so continuous that a person could read by it, which she did as a joke for Orren while they were lying in bed.

On Saturday late in the afternoon, while Orren sat at the dining table working figures and turning and searching the sky out the window every few minutes and Aloma stood on the front porch, barely protected against the slanting wind so that her hips were dry but her bare legs were slashed with rain, she saw a funnel cloud. One second all she could see was the rain slacking down by the road but still falling heavy at the house where she stood, and the next second the funnel appeared. By the time she reckoned what it was, she was too stunned to move. It was not large, it stretched from the low clouds to the grass that appeared unearthly green now in its saturation under the glaze of urine-yellow light that sickened the sky. It shimmied and snaked there, it seemed to advance and still Aloma could not move her feet and with an impassivity that would later startle her, she saw straight through the funnel to the trees on the other side and she knew suddenly, as though the thought had been gifted to her, that the wrecking blast of the funnel cloud was also God's creation along with the dirt of the farm and her stricken face and all the rest of the living too. And that scared her properly and she moved back then in two giant steps, but as she reached for the door and Orren's name was already forming in the stretch of her mouth, the cloud swung out to the side like the trunk of an elephant, and then spitting out the grass and branches it had drawn into it, it swirled wanly up into the clouds.

After that, she made Orren bring the television up from the small house — which he did, getting soaked to the skin again — so they could put it on the bedroom floor with the sound turned down just to watch the weather. If any more tornadoes came, they could flee with barely any warning around the side of the house to the root cellar. Long after Orren had fallen asleep against the soprano scream of the wind along the eaves of the house, she lay in the blue-lit dark watching the screen across his body. She wondered if all men could sleep this soundly under duress, fast to trust their own bodies and closing their eyes to everything else. But she did not know any other men, had not seen the way they slept, and she wondered as she looked at the screen how it would feel to have someone else sleep beside her, or be inside her even, and if that would speak to her happiness, which she felt lay unborn within her. She looked at Orren, the back of his head and his curved shoulder where he had drawn his right arm into his chest. Then she stifled the feeling by scooting up behind him, allowing her body to follow perfectly the line of his and then blocking out the blue flickering of the television and the living storm by pressing her head into his shoulder and the pillow. She lay there for a long time and tried not to think. Finally she fell into a wary sleep and in the morning the rains had stopped and she went to church.

* * *

After the service that resounded with amens and prayer like hollering, Aloma walked across the parking lot to her truck saying goodbye to the people she passed. Bell walked up behind her. She knew it was him when she heard or felt rather the coarse gravel of his voice as he spoke to the very same people she had just passed. She had reached her truck and placed her hand on the door handle, pretending she did not know he was there, feeling foolish even as she did it, when he said, Miss Aloma.

She turned.

Before you go, he said and he reached into the pocket of his trousers and fished among the coins that chinked and cuffed there until he found what he was looking for. I got something for you, he said.

What? she said and she could not keep her voice from sounding pleased.

Well, you come in here every day, he said. You're more regular than this clock — and he shook his wrist so that his silver watch rattled — and you are a paid employee of this church, the only employee. You know I don't get a thing to preach. I figured I might could give you a key to the building. He held out his hand in which a small gold key flashed like a wink and she stretched out her own hand and he passed it into her palm so that his fingertips brushed hers as he looked at her and said, I trust you. She wrapped her hand in a fist around the key so that its teeth bit her flesh.

Now you can practice anytime you care to, but better not at night, I reckon. And then he laughed, as though he'd said something funny, only he stopped abruptly and it was that laugh, and the awkward way in which he would not let himself do it, that filled Aloma with knowing. She looked up at him and said in not much more than a whisper, Thank you so much, Bell. And because he heard his first name in her mouth, he blushed.

Abruptly he turned to go, but then stopped, hesitating for a moment so that she did not know if he was coming or going and then he turned to face her again. He did not close the two steps he had opened between them. He studied the ground before her feet.

I got a thing to ask you, he said.

What's that? she said.

He put his hands on his hips. Well, he said and he looked up now, not at her, but above her toward the sky, the way he sometimes did when he preached, as though God could be sought out in the rafters. Well, the other day when we all . . . when we did the picnic —

She blinked and it felt as though something very heavy were clinging to her lids.

Well, I seen you drive by, he said. I seen you drive by and not stop. And I just, I figure I just questioned why that was. He looked at her straight now, finally.

For a moment she only pressed the inside of her lower teeth with her tongue.

I don't know. I guess I'm just shy, she said finally, and she hated herself powerfully as she said it, for it was not true exactly, but a seduction by meekness. She put her head down, not in reserve as it appeared.

Well, he said again, it's too bad is all you didn't stop and talk. Spend time with the church. Aloma remained where she was with her head down, but when he didn't move, only stood there staring at her, she raised her head. His eyes were so direct she felt she could not match them, but sought instead the smaller details of his face, the straight nose, heavy winged brows, very black. She was not aware of smiling.

Bell Ray, a voice said and Bell turned and Aloma looked around the block of his shoulder. His mother stood ten feet away, and though there were people milling all around her, she passed the curious impression that she stood singularly amidst them. Her Bible was clutched in her hand and pressed to her small lowhung chest.

Yes, Mother, Bell said.

Bell, I need you, she said and she did not look at Aloma when she said this, only at Bell. He took a step toward his mother and then, as if remembering suddenly that he'd been speaking with Aloma, he faced her again and said, It would please me if you'd practice to your heart's content. And then he turned and followed his mother into the crowd so that the people surrounded him and Aloma could see no more than the back of his dark and sunlit head.

★ ★ ★

Aloma found that the harder she worked around the house, the more she assuaged the stab of that slight pleasure, and it worked so well she forgot it happened at all. She already rose with Orren in the mornings to fix him breakfast and brew coffee, but now she walked out of the house with him and went down to the barn where she mixed the scratch with oyster shell as Orren had shown her and scattered it across the hay-strewn barn floor. She couldn't say that she enjoyed it, but after a few weeks, it didn't seem like such a chore, though it was a pity to be confronted with such stupidity as the chickens managed to reveal on a daily basis. When Orren rebuilt a small ramp that led from the coop to the floor, a laying hen fell off the ramp while walking up it and no amount of pecking and hunting helped her find it again because she was under it. So Aloma picked her up — and she hated to touch the chickens and feel the unexpected, distressing strength of their sinewy wings corrugated by veins and feathers — and placed the hen back on the ramp so she could fall off again. Eventually she resettled the hen's nest on the barn floor. But aside from that, she found that she actually liked searching out the eggs and holding them, smooth and even in her hand — the fawn brown carapace of the eggs far more beautiful than the white, she thought — before she basketed them in the hem of her shirt. She studied the morning light as it forced itself through the pocked and splintered wood boards of the batten walls so that it shot through in silty bands of white like roughspun silk. It caught and lit the barn sediment as morning sun lights the mist and bugs that hover over the skin of a still river. And her walk back up to the house with the eggs cradled in her shirt and against her pale and rounded belly was a very fine walk. With the morning barely born and the new sun low, before the ugly countenance of her enclosure was featured by broad daylight, she felt good.

To her surprise, she found that she was learning to clean and cook with the speed of a woman who'd done it her whole life. The linseed oil on her hands became her workaday perfume. She always meant to go down to the new house to clean and organize — she had not really seen it since the day they took the kitchen supplies back up to the old house, when she had seen very little beyond its low-ceilinged kitchen. After that, she had been consumed with the cleaning and organizing of the big house and it was an endless task, really. Every time she turned her back, new dust collected and gray mice nested again and old closets began to smell like wet shoes so that she never had a moment to think about the new house at all and soon accepted that she would get down there only when she was able. It had been a long time since she'd even wondered when that would be. And while she cleaned, while she scrubbed and made plans for the mildewed upstairs bath, which was inhospitable — that's what she had taken to calling it — she was so lost in the passing daydreams as they played across her mind, she failed to notice the figure of Bell showing up with determined frequency until he became a kind of constant unnoticed guest. And even when she returned to the church as she did for longer periods now, sometimes for up to four hours a day, she did not see — or chose to ignore — how her eyes sought immediately for Bell's truck in the parking lot and how she played not quite as pertly, not as accurately, when he was not in the building. Her mind wandered when he was not hidden away in the privacy of his office so that she sometimes found herself stopped in the middle of a song she had memorized five years prior, and even rising from the piano in a fit of unrest to wander down a row of pews, stare out a window at the churchyard, the trees that lined one side of the parking lot, the sky beyond. The music had drawn her to this place, to this church, but now she looked out the windows more and more and played less and less. Only when Bell was not there. Otherwise, she drew all the force of her concentration to bear on the music before her and thought again how one day soon she would audition for a music program and then Orren would be ready to go with her, or maybe not . . . These were her thoughts on a Tuesday afternoon when Bell — who sometimes paused in the doorway to watch her play for a few moments but never came inside — walked into the sanctuary. He stood a few feet from the door, closer to the door than to her, and watched as she played.

He waited until she was done and said, What's that you played just now?

A Mozart sonata, she said.

He walked up to the piano and looked down at the keys. He leaned down and pressed one and the pitch sounded, substantial and unadorned, on the air. I never learned to play, he said. I ought to have.

Oh, she said, did you want to?

We got a piano, he said, straightening up again. We still got it, though it can't a been tuned for twenty years, I reckon. It's beautiful, a special old piano. My grandfather bought it and there wasn't nothing like it around here. He bought it for my grandmother Lily. He shook his head. Nobody had pianos back then. Just devil's fiddles, he said and smiled, glancing at her, then back down at the piano again. It's carved too. I don't know who did that, but the legs are carved — and it's done good too, somebody who knew what they were doing. The top is carved too.

The top, she wondered.

Yes.

It sounds kind of unusual. I bet it's pretty, she said.

And when she said that, Bell said, Would

you like to see it? and she made a play at hesitating for a moment and then with her face turned up so that the light of the window shone on her and deepened her eyes, she said, Yes.

He drove her out in the old car with the fancy fins, the one she had seen when she first came to the church asking for a job. His land was small, or at least the planted part of the land was no more than a few acres, just a plot of tobacco he pulled and sold at auction.

If I didn't preach that church, he said, I'd farm the whole place, all the way down to the house like they used to. That's how they used to do it. But when Daddy started to reverend that church, it got to be too much. We let a whole bunch go fallow.

But they don't even pay you, she said.

Nah, can't take no pay to preach. That ain't right. And I lose money here to do it too, but we get by fine. Daddy always did it that way, I do the same.

The house where he lived with his mother stood much closer to the ridge than her house so that it reminded her of the school, the way it had nested in morning shadows. It made her a little earthsick to look on it. The tobacco rowed out before it on long raised beds and the fallow fields whiskered with tall grasses that shook and tangled with the wind that rose off the road.

I can't figure why they built so close to the wall, he said. That ain't safe at all. I got a second cousin in Grundy whose wife got killed when a boulder come down off the mountain and crashed right through the living room right in front of them. He shook his head. I always figured if I got rich — God forbid it — I'd rebuild out in that field — he pointed to a fallow field — that way we'd get more easterly light. That would be good for Mother. Morning light is good for the soul. I believe that.

Mrs. Johnson was in the house when they went in. She opened the door for them when they had barely stepped up onto the porch, as if she'd been hovering behind the door with her arthritic hand on the knob.

Hello, Mrs. Johnson, said Aloma and the woman nodded and smiled the smallest smile ever mustered by a human face.

I brought Aloma to see the piano, Bell said and Aloma wondered if his mother also caught the way he no longer called her miss, and from the long sideways look she cast him, it appeared she had. It's over here, he said. Aloma followed him into a living room so full of furniture and bric-a-brac that Aloma's eyes did not know where to rest. Photographs and newspaper clippings in frames covered the

194

walls, plates and whittlings of tiny animals arranged in crowds on every shelf, pillows and blankets piled on every soft surface. All neat, all orderly, but no end to the heaped and hoarded possessions. The piano was the only unadorned object in the room. She stepped to it and stared at the complexion of its wood, blackish and vein-crackled with age, with carvings winding up the legs and across its top. She had expected it to be rough-hewn like the little whittlings all over the room — done by what appeared to be a young hand — but these were smooth and each line traced a sinuous curve. She ran her hand across the top. Bell lifted the cover then and showed her the keys, which had yellowed so that the grain ringed darkly on the surface. She pressed four keys in arpeggiation and the sound bloated out, the pitches sagging and unclean. She stood for a moment with her lips puckered out in disappointment, one eyebrow peevishly risen. She did not look up.

Been a long time since it was tuned, Bell said and laughed a laugh that threatened her temper suddenly.

Why not?

Ain't a body to play it, said his mother, who until that moment had been standing in the doorway, watching silently, her hands curled at her sides.

I got a photograph upstairs of my grandfather with this thing. Hold up a minute, Bell said and he turned the corner past his mother and his feet sounded up the staircase.

His mother did not move, but she said, Was you at the church?

Yes, said Aloma and looked down at the piano again coolly. I was practicing piano.

Ever day, the woman said. It was not a question, but Aloma said, Yes, as though it was. She suddenly became sensible of the multiple clocks ticking in the room. Then the woman said, Where at do your people hail from?

From Cady Station.

I can't hear that in your talk.

Is that right, said Aloma and looked at her with a pointed expression that the woman could not miss. Then, as though the old woman were not in the room, she turned her back on her to look at the pictures on the nearest wall.

How come you to be here? said the woman to her back, but then Bell's feet returned again to the stairs and he was in the room with a framed photograph in his hand of a very thin and tall man dressed in black standing beside the piano, which bore the high sheen of youth then. Aloma felt another sudden flash of irritation as she took the photo out of his hands — at his cankerous mother, at Bell for bringing her here, at herself for coming, and most of all at this wracked piano, a perfect beauty rotted in its shell. She could not understand why everyone let the best things pass into disrepair and she would have thought Bell a better man than that, a man who could care especially for something — a piano, an old house, a woman. She looked up at him. It's getting late, she said, handing the photo back, and she prayed silently that his mother would say nothing further, which she did not, she only stared and chewed at her lip and stood aside as they left the house.

★ ★ ★

The bright outside did little to relieve her. She followed Bell as he folded his frame into the old car and cranked the engine. They passed a mud-spattered late-model truck where it stood parked like a mechanical afterthought in the middle of the mudded front lane, which was patchworked with tire tracks running the length of the tobacco field. In the rearview mirror, she watched the small house recede with its hanging baskets, the small dark figure of his mother, the ridge wall beyond. In the dayward tilt of the woman's body thrusting her pinched face into the space before her, Aloma was reminded of Bell, the way he stood on the edge of the front pews as he preached as if he were standing on the prow of a boat looking out. She glanced at him to consider the resemblance.

It's funny how you look like your mother, she said.

Funny how?

Well, not funny . . . interesting.

He shot her a quizzical look.

I just think it's interesting when people look like other people. I don't think there's a person in the whole world that looks like me.

Oh, he said. I see. Then, after a moment's silence, I'm sure your mother looked like you.

She shrugged.

I'm sure she was pretty like you.

Aloma turned her face to the passing land and screwed up her lip, didn't acknowledge him. She thought of the piano, she did not feel generous.

It must be tough not to have your folks, Bell said.

No.

Come on now, Aloma. He smiled. You don't got to act tough.

No, she said, stiff. I never even think about

them. I don't feel anything about it one way or the other way.

I don't believe that, he said, not for one blessed minute.

Well, it's true.

Now, I can't believe it's natural to feel that way, Bell said. Hearts don't do that of their own according, it takes some kind of effort to make them stop behaving properly. I hear you play your piano every day, you know. I trust you got right feeling.

Aloma bit her lip and drew her brows together. She made a face out the window that he couldn't see, irritated that he had made a press for softness, like a thumb testing fruit. But she felt guilt for her meanness too, she didn't know what was wrong with her and thought, in her tangled mind, she wasn't made like other women. There was some softness in her, but it was so deep in a kind of acquired bitter that it took another bitter to divine it, like an auger cuts through solid rock to force the seam.

Well, what if I really don't have the right feeling? Aloma said then.

Bell laughed, but she didn't join him. He looked at her.

How do I get that? she said.

Well, he said and cleared his throat. It might sound kinda contrary, but I don't think looking inside for a feeling is nearly ever the answer. It's looking out.

What's that mean? she said, all suspicion.

Well, it seems to me the more attention you spend on the folks around you, the more right feeling you have even for your own self. Seems like the opposite might should be true — turn your mind on your own heart to straighten it out — but that ain't how I see it. Am I making sense?

She smiled wanly at him, but her smile was troubled by a distrust directed as much at herself as at him.

Hey, he said suddenly. Don't let's go to the church just yet. Let me show you something special.

Alright, she agreed, feeling the rub of her conscience, but not caring.

Bell drove toward the eastern side of the county where the flatter sheeting of the bluegrass met the hills. Here Spade's Knob stood, a steep breast of limestone seduced out from the body of the foothills, it swelled anciently green over limestone over thin coal and fossilized remains. It rose rank-grown and shaggy with thick midsummer vegetation.

It's just up this east slope, he said and his car whined in first gear along its uprise and the low-lying farms diminished as they ascended, their tree-lined fields flashing green between breaks in the blacker green of the mountain trees. Bell slowed a third of the way up the mountain at a sloping hillside graveyard, its draped graves rioting with color against the unchecked green of the hillside. He parked so the car tilted crazily, half on the road, half on the hill.

This is my favorite place, Bell said. They walked out among the tiny spread of graves, Aloma a few feet ahead of him. Each headstone stood decorated with wreaths of fabric flowers — their cheer artificial beauty fresh and unfaded, notecards and photographs in transparent bags taped to the carved stones. On a date of 1882, a lei. Or a Confederate cavalryman, his furrowed horse with its legs outstretched in a dead run, its pasterns limp as lady-hands. The dead in their graves lay ordered with their soles to the distant ridges, the earth collapsed into the narrow space of their coffin boxes. Aloma thought of them, bodies less substantial than even their names in death, no more animated than a stone. She breathed sharp over them, over those absented bones, and smelled the hot green August on the verge of turning. But the season was not done, the smell of the hillside was redolent with honeysuckle and grass and some of the heavy tartness of ripe pears. She looked around her, saw no pear trees, turned toward the sheer wall of the mountain behind the graves, the oaks blanketed with an impenetrable draping of kudzu, as if they — Aloma and Bell — stood with their feet on the edge of some fantastical evergreen bed. Bell pointed away from the mountain wall to where the distant farms lay between Spade's Knob and the thick succession of coaled ridges, the buckled-up crust darked by trees. They went on and on without surcease.

That's about the prettiest thing I ever saw in my life. He sighed. Aloma looked at it balefully, she had borne herself out of its sucking folds. Its beauty was a thing hard to stand. She looked down as far south as she was able, but could not see Orren's farm.

I mowed all this for the Ather family when I was a just a kid. Easy work. Everybody comes and does their own graves near about every week. Folks are good like that here, still. When I was in Lexington, all the graveyards up there are just empty and gray and not a flower on any stones. That's shameful, I think.

When were you in Lexington? she said, surprised.

I went up there to college for not too long, six months maybe.

You quit?

Yeah, I did quit.

Why?

He sighed and with both hands wiped the sweat from either side of his broad face. Homesick, I guess.

She smiled.

Not really, he said. Just fancy, silly. Too much learning and not a bit of common sense. I never heard so many people talk so much to say nothing. Got so I couldn't get out of bed. So I came back home. Never felt no need to go back.

I'd like to go up there someday, she said.

No, you couldn't have stood it.

How do you know that? she said, sharp. He looked at her in surprise then, eyes outlining the shape of her face and settling on the veiled argument of her eyes. He paused at length before he said, Well, maybe not. He crossed his arms over his chest and contemplated her, and sensing a looming shift, she started to turn aside, but he said first, There's something funny about you.

No, not really, she said, deflecting.

Yes, he said and he looked out to the mountains and then at her again. You seem real sweet, but sometimes you . . .

She looked at him, trapped like a horse in its thills, her eyes full of false innocence.

. . . Sometimes you got a cagey thing about

you. Like you can't decide if you want to run off or get took in.

There was a long moment before she realized that she was released and then she began to laugh, hilarity poised on the pinpoint of her fear. You make me sound like a stray dog, she said when finally she came up for air and he watched her with a confused, unwilling grin growing on his own face.

Well, he said, and then as she started up again, Yeah, but who you got in the world, really? and laughing, she pretended it was a joke and not the serious inquiry it was and impotent in his feeling, he stood beside her and let her lie through her laughter. Not happily, but gently, he stooped and picked up the mown desiccated grasses and threw them at her and she laughed and laughed in relief that he only found her a strange thing, but not deceitful yet.

★　★　★

The next morning when Aloma stepped into the barn she found chickens scattered on the barn floor and thought for a second, irritably, that they must be playing dead. She said, Hey, out loud and none of them moved.

Oh shit, she said. She whirled around to find Orren, who had left the house thirty

204

minutes before her own sleepy shuffle down to the barn. She heard the tractor from where she stood, he was still tilling up the southern end of the fallow field. When she turned back around, she hoped against hope the chickens might be standing up, but they were still dead.

Oh trouble, she said and she ran out of the barn, scaling the pasture fence without bothering for the gate, ran with her arms flailing across the crown of the tobacco field and into the fallow field of damp beds. Orren saw her coming and she raised her hand, but he did not cut the motor. He watched her come running, her shirt coming loose from the waistband of her jeans, her ponytail shaking down.

Some of the chickens are dead! she yelled.

What? he called. She pointed at the steering column of the tractor and he cut the motor and it fell with a whinny and a low shudder.

Some of the chickens got killed.

How many? he said.

Seven, I think.

Oh fuck, he said and swung down off the tractor, half walked a moment and then ran with Aloma trailing behind him to the barn where he stood and surveyed the chickens lying, yellow scaled legs stiffed out in a manner that was funny, some reluctant part of Aloma's brain knew, but she was not laughing, neither was he.

Oh shit, Orren said and bent down and eyeballed a chicken at close range before he nudged it with his boot. If we got a sickness in here, we'll lose ever last one of them if seven is dead already.

Oh no, Aloma said. She looked around at the other chickens, terrified now they would drop dead in her sight. Four sat nested. One journeyed, head bobbing epileptically, among the dead.

Orren crossed to the broody and her early chicks. The bright chicks darted around the darker hen, who stood as Orren approached, her black eyes pierced the air around her. Orren backed away slowly and gazed down again to peer at a dead chicken and then, with a sharp motion, stooped to his haunches to feel with a flat hand the barn floor around the carcass.

Is this feed wet?

Aloma looked at him blankly. He stalked to the feed bag, but while he did this his eyes never left hers and his body moved with a conviction that made her breath catch so Aloma had to physically restrain herself from reaching out to keep him. She knew already from his body, she always did. She was lifting her hands up to her throat in despair when Orren looked down into the feed bag and said, Oh, for fucksake, Aloma, the goddamn feed is wet!

Oh, she said, her voice like a whistle.

What the hell's it doing over at the door for? She had never seen his eyes so wide.

I couldn't see it where you had it over in the crib! Aloma cried. I couldn't see anything! It was — She just stopped then, miserable. She glared down at the chickens. What kind of animal ate ruined feed? It had rained into the barn door a bit and how could she have known that —

Wet feed does *that* to a chicken, Orren said and he pointed at the chickens, made stupider than they naturally were by death, Aloma thought smally as she followed, unwillingly, his finger.

Oh, she said, more moan than word. Waiting for more, Orren just stood there. Then he raised one hand up to his forehead with an odd yelping sound and, barely restrained, tugged his hair straight up as though he would pull it out by the roots. Then he stalked to the stall and from a wall of long-handled tools, yanked off a wide broom.

I'll feed the motherfucking hens myself, he said.

Aloma's head snapped up. Don't cuss at me! she screamed and then she ran from the barn and he let her go. But she made it only five yards before she turned abruptly so the dust fanned out from her feet and she ran back to where Orren had already begun to sweep up the damp feed. She yanked the broom out of his hands before he even realized she was there and began furiously sweeping at the floor so that the feed and the hay and the droppings swung up into the air and she accidentally struck one of the hens that, was still living and it shrieked and flew into the rafters in a storm of feathers and drifting sediment.

Give it here, Aloma, Orren said, calmer now, reaching around her with both arms.

No, she said and jerked the broom away with one hand and used the other to strike Orren at the rise of his chest so he had to step back to escape her. Then she swept the floor with jerking motions, but slightly subdued now so that the sodden feed — what was left of it — could be gathered and thrown away in the trash.

Fine, said Orren behind her and he walked back to the stall and took up another broom and they swept the barn, but with their backs to each other so that Orren could not see the tears in Aloma's eyes.

Later that day, Aloma counted out the money she had earned from playing piano. It was not much, but she drove it down to the feed store and stood at the back landing where she knew bags of feed and mulch were tossed into the waiting beds of trucks. She waited, but no one appeared. She walked into the building and a small bell made a large pronouncement behind her. Along a shallow gully in the floor worn by men's boots past the dusty shelves, she walked. She tasted the dust in the air and the faded inoffensive smell of animals. Her face was careful and muted when she reached the register. Two men stood there, one ringing the other out. The clerk, bald as a finial, looked up, and before his shy male eyes wavered, she said, I need to buy chickens. The second man shoved his billfold into his back pocket and glanced over his shoulder, looked away, and looked again. Then he turned fully around and leaned back on the counter, his legs spread wide. He did not have red hair, but his face was spattered with freckles.

The clerk leaned to one side to peer around the other man's shoulder and said, Ma'am, you gotta mail-order chicks. They come in a box. How many you want?

Seven chickens for laying, she said. It

sounded like a question.

The man leaning on the counter did not have to open his mouth to speak to her, it was already slung open. Hey, if you want chickens, I got me some chickens. Chicks or laying hens or whatever you want. Yes-huh, I got a whole mess of em. I can't hardly stand the sight of em. I don't even eat no eggs neither. I get sicker'n . . . His head swiveled toward the clerk. Shoot. I get ill. His voice was more holler than talk.

The man behind the counter coughed up a laugh. Don't cull no sick hens off on no girl. Ma'am, he said.

How much? she said to the man with the mouth at the ready and fishing money out of her pocket, she held her palm out and up. Is this enough?

Shoot, said the man.

That a get you more hens than eggs you care to eat, the clerk said.

I need seven, she said.

Who you sell your eggs to? the clerk said, but the man interrupted, Well, I got birds if you want birds. I got me a big old place. I bet you seen it if you ever drove out up on 52. You ever drove out that way? I got a big set of land, I got a big house. I got more'n most can handle, he said and he turned back toward the clerk and Aloma saw him wink — both eyes winked when one tried — and he lifted his hand to the clerk in a three-fingered salute. Aloma traipsed after him out of the store and in the half-moon mirror above the door saw the clerk wipe at his nose with mild disinterest as he watched her go. Outside, the man said, Now, I'm about two miles down and left on 52. First place, it's a big place, can't nobody miss it. You'll see. Well, it's just about the biggest place. Tobacco, mostly. Costy. Ropes me in a ton a cash. I'm fixing to build me a new house. He turned his face to one side, spat, and wiped two rosin-brown droplets from his lip. When Aloma said nothing, only smiled a girlish smile, he tossed his paper bag on the front seat of his truck and placed one booted foot on the driver's-side running board. He said, Well honey, don't get lost. Stay right close behind me. I drive faster'n I should, but I ain't never even got no ticket yet. I ain't never been shut down, not yet once. And I don't stop for nothing but sin. I don't know if you can keep up, I don't take it easy not even for no girl. And then as she moved to her truck and he saw her empty bed, he said, Hey, you ain't got no cages.

And she said, Oh. No, no.

That's alright, he said. I reckon I can haul em to your place. He situated the tobacco in his lip. Where you live at? I bet you I know it.

Fourteen Burnt Ridge Road, she said. Under the ridge. It's a white house.

Shoot, he said. That old place? And she saw the play of his thoughts so clear it was as if his head was split open for display and he went to speak but stopped so he stuttered, a grin spirited his face. He only said, That ain't too big a place.

You can't see all the land from the road, she said.

Well, huh, he said. Maybe. Still, I'd not want no bottomland like that'n. My papaw lived out Sunday Holler — you know where that's at, when they had them rains back in . . . Shoot, I can't turn up exactly when all it was, but they was washed out and when that big slurry come down the mountain, they swimmed out on bedsteads and barrels —

It's plenty big for me, she said and he said, Well, is that right, and his lip pouched out, interrupted from his tobacco. She smiled a downcasting apology, jiggled her keys from a fingertip. Then he swung into his seat and said, Hup, like his truck was a horse and he started up his engine hard, gunning. Well, come and catch me if you can, he said and he drove as fast as he had promised. She followed him down the winding creek road and out 52 where the mountains flattened to a hazing blue in her rearview. They pulled into a gravel drive and passed two white trailers and a two-story house, behind it stood a new gambrel-roofed barn. The man parked backward with the bed of his truck facing the shadowed barn interior. Once out of his truck, he turned her way and made a show of stretching so his shirt pulled up. She saw the furring line of hair below his waist. He looked at her as she slid out from behind the wheel and he grinned, nodded as if she'd said something he liked, then he turned into his barn, reaching back once to pat his worn Skoal ring. Up in the mow, he found his cages, which he handed down to her and then he half slid, half jumped down and in a flurry, he wrestled a few hens, checking them first and choosing which to keep and which to discard, holding each one up toward Aloma and giving each a little prize shake so they squawked in alarm. Watch yourself, darlin, he said and then he battled them into their cages — rougher than he needed to, she thought — and they fought with their scratching skinny legs and their hateful eyes until seven were caught and caged.

Glad to be shed of em is what, he said when he was done. Them's good layers. I just got too many of em. He wiped his hands on his jeans. I ain't got time to mess with no chickens and I can't even eat no eggs. Makes me ill. And ain't nobody round to eat em 'cept my old granny, he said and he winked with both eyes again, the one lagging fractionally behind the other. Ain't a body here, he said again. Not a one, not a one. I ain't got a thing to have.

She surveyed the land behind her out the broad door of the barn. She could see the border fencing in two directions, but she said, Yeah, but you've got a real big place, and he gave a whooping laugh, a dilute rebel chirp, and said, You are right. You are right. She got herself a poker face, but she calls it like she sees it. Then, with the chickens loaded into cages and the cages loaded into the bed of his truck, which Aloma saw now was jacked up a little higher than was really necessary, they rolled out of the farm. Aloma followed him again as he led the way back up 52 and down the winding roads to Burnt Ridge. And as they rolled up the gravel of the drive, his truck raised two horsetails of dust. Little blossom-white feathers fluttered out of the bed of his truck and up and over Aloma's truck. When they crested the drive, Aloma saw Orren appear on the front porch, one hand raised to his eyes. Nearing the house, the man leaned out of his driver's-side window and looked back at her, grinning, and

Aloma waved for him to stop instead of continuing on down to the barn. He parked, but when the man suddenly saw Orren he did not turn off his truck but left it puttering in neutral, sat there for a moment, spat once, looked back at Aloma once, and then stepped out and put his hands to his lean hips.

Haddy, said the man, his voice saltless now, and Orren only nodded at him and they both looked at Aloma, at each other once more, and then at the chickens.

I bought you new chickens, Aloma said, leaning against the front bumper of her truck. New used chickens.

I sold em to her, the man said, trying unsuccessfully to look at both of them at the same time, his eyebrows working. Orren stepped down off the porch with his hand out. Orren Fenton, he said.

Caudill, Chris Caudill, he said and they shook. I just . . . He made a vague gesture in Aloma's direction. I got a place out . . . 52. Now them hens . . . Now, a couple them's bantam and I don't know if you was wanting em, but —

Size don't speak to strength, said Orren.

The man cleared his throat. Now, no, he said.

Did my wife make you come out all this way? said Orren and Aloma looked at him hard from where she stood, but she bit her tongue.

Well, said the man and he cleared his throat. Then he palmed his forehead for a moment and looked vaguely surprised as if he hadn't expected it to still be there. He glanced at his truck. She ain't had no cages to hold em. She ain't wanted no chicks neither, just growed hens. Now, I sold em to her.

Well, sorry for your extra trouble, said Orren. I had no idea whatsoever she was fixing to get hens. The man just shrugged with both shoulders and together they unloaded the cages from the bed of the truck and set them on the porch, the chickens fretting, some of them winging up to batter the tops of the cages, rattling them. When they were done, Orren patted around in his pockets for a few spare dollars, but the man just held up his hands and said, Aw no, we're level. No need. You just park them cages at the feed store and I'll fetch em when I'm able.

I apologize for that, Orren said again.

That ain't no problem, like I said, said the man. And he turned to go, but then paused and looked at Aloma for a moment, both his eyebrows raised and one half of his mouth curling into a brief puckish grin and Orren saw it and Aloma straightened up, pleased. Orren crossed his arms. Aloma said, Thank you again for driving all the way out here for me. I really like your truck. Orren, she said with a dumb small smile, do you think we could get one that big? And Orren just looked at her without blinking and the man grinned and said, Bye now, and got in his truck and drove away, gunning once and then again. Orren watched her watching him go.

That was right fucking cute, he said.

Yeah well, she snapped, don't call me your wife till I am your wife, and then she stalked past him onto the front porch. When she reached the door, he said, Where'd you get the cash at for all these hens?

From playing piano, she said without turning around, and not seeing the look on his face only heightened the satisfaction of knowing she had taken him by surprise.

★ ★ ★

He did let her feed the chickens again. She knew he would. He was tight-mouthed for a few days, but when she went ahead and walked to the barn one morning, checking the feed compulsively with her hand to make for certain it was dry, he did not stop her. They didn't speak of it again. She had bought the chickens, after all. They were now hers to kill.

She did not even realize that the first week of September had arrived until Orren announced to her one morning — his relief convenient to read in the easing of his brow — that he'd always liked a first harvest to usher in the fall and she looked to their kitchen calendar and saw that it was so. Three months had passed since the day she had arrived with her boxes of scores and her white nightgown in its paper catalog packaging, a brown bag she had folded and saved in one of Emma's upstairs drawers. Her nightgown had now been laundered many times. The white ribbon that twisted and tied in a bow over her breasts was frayed and slightly yellowed.

I'm fixing to get some men for today, Orren said.

Where at? she said, casting out over the gold-green tobacco, the darkened soil.

Hansonville. On the road. They come for the pullings.

He turned and looked down toward the tawnied field and she eyed his back. She had half a mind to offer her hands to him for the day, but instead she tapped her teeth pensively behind him. She wanted something from him first. It was true she didn't know the first thing about cutting tobacco, she'd already proved herself more liability than help, but still it was the asking that she was waiting for. She grasped the weak power of waiting for him to come to her.

When Orren left for town, Aloma decided that, despite the heat, she would bake for most of the day in order to pass the time until she went to the church. She set up fans in the kitchen windows that drew the hot air out and read her scores line by line as though they were books while the breads rose and browned. But her spirit was aimless, she stood repeatedly all day, walking to the back door to gaze down to the field where Orren and the men stooped and cut the yellowed butt and middle leaves, piercing the stalks on the sticks so the field was lined with rows of miniature husked tepees. Stray leaves scattered on the soil between the rows, one of the men returned and collected them, dusting them with his gloved hands. At the southern edge of the field the curing shed stood in wait, its wide black doors rolled open. In the early afternoon, when the heat of the baking punished the room, Aloma walked out of the house and stood shielded from sight by the withes of the willow and she watched them work. Orren stood and pointed, they conversed in a distant silent circle. She wondered then if Bell was cutting his own harvest this week. It seemed likely, the butts of his tobacco were already broad and browned when she had visited. She would have to ask him. Aloma lingered a moment more under the willow, looked back once over her shoulder as she retreated to the house with her hands in her pockets. She had only wanted him to ask.

By three she had already haunted every room a half dozen times so she abandoned her baking and drove to the church and she let herself in. The building was quiet, empty. Her playing echoed in the room and she waited impatiently for Bell to come, but when he did, he entered through the back and went straight to his office without stopping. She listened to the single clapping sound his door made when it closed. Aloma waited for a minute or two to see if he would appear in the doorway, but when he did not, she tried again to focus on the keyboard, but her will was sapped and she could not sit still. She wanted to go back to Bell's office and speak to him — about what she didn't care, about anything really — but she didn't. She just forced her fingers to the keys until she felt that the music jammed like a machine whose gears had caught and she had to stop herself from bringing her hands down on the keyboard in frustration. She was gripped by a surging restlessness. Her ears strained for any sounds from Bell's office. Then finally she shot up from the piano, angry at Bell's silence, or perhaps at Orren, and she grabbed her scores and drove home.

Behind the big house, the men were still in the fields, tents of tobacco windrowed where the flush yellow plants had been, the stalks cut and wilting on sticks in the sun. The men were bent in their cutting and sticking so that Aloma could not distinguish between them. She could not even determine which one was Orren until he straightened up and removed his cap to wipe the sweat from above his eyes. Then he returned the cap to his head and turned away again into the anonymous gesture of his labor.

Aloma was hot and silent as the kitchen she stood in. She made roast beef sandwiches without singing to herself or otherwise uttering a sound. There was no point in wiping away the sweat from her lip or from her chest where it ran in the thinnest stream between her breasts. As she carried a platter of sandwiches and a pitcher of stirred lemonade down to the field, Orren and one of the hands made their way to the curing barn, their unbuttoned shirts trailing from the waistbands of their trousers so Aloma could see the sun-marked working of their backs.

The third man, fanning himself with a stray tobacco leaf, stood and watched them go. He buttoned up his shirt, unhurried, when he saw Aloma coming down the row, her skirt whispering against her legs as she came, the pitcher chittering on the tray.

Ma'am.

She nodded at him, took in the sunbeat face and freckled lips, his cigarette-drawn mouth. When he turned his fair colorless head, she saw through his various missing teeth to the dark interior of his mouth.

He took one sandwich, said, You his girl?

Aloma looked to the curing barn, took her time. Yeah.

Well, he ain't much to look at, but he's hell for stout.

Aloma laughed, she couldn't help it.

It's a tough job for that boy, the man said.

To harvest, she said.

The whole bit. He made a gesture with one finger lifted off the bread of his sandwich, to indicate the whole of the farm.

Aloma looked around, her brows knitted together. Yeah, the whole bit, she conceded. Her eyes found Orren inside the barn fiddling with a yardrod peering into the rafters, and when he reached up with his arms spread so his body opened up momentarily like something blooming, she was afflicted with the memory of how he had been when she first met him as he stood with his cap on, looking at her sideways like he knew he was going to have her before he even did, just because he still believed good things could happen. Her mouth slid open.

The man stood watching her face, the tobacco leaf idle in his hand. Tough job for a girl too. Just a mite little thing. It a wear the living out of you.

Her eyes refocused on his. No, I'm mean enough for it.

He laughed a phlegmy smoker's laugh. Most girls is mean, he said. Right to hear one say it, though. Then he said, He told us his people died. That's a mess. He looked around them at the cut plants. Got to be done, I reckon.

It's got to be done, she parroted flatly, looking down at the bowing severed plants, but even as she said it, she thought, But why?

The man only nodded his head, Well, sure, sure. He done good. He's a good boy. And she looked at him directly then, not smiling, not seeing him either, but turning slightly so that she could take in the curing barn before her and the house to her right and she moved away from the man with a faint expression on her face. She left the sandwiches and lemonade between the rows and began to walk toward the house. Behind her the fair-headed man said, But not too mean, missy. Not too mean . . .

Aloma walked back up the hill to the house. Once there, the stillness and the relative order of the place only rattled her unease. She moved from room to room, her motions out of joint. Strange that she could want to be here and at the church at the same time, and yet feel that no matter where she found herself, she would be nowhere. Her heart was chilled, but her hands felt to be in a fever as she scooped up the keys to her truck to drive back to the church. But with the keys in her hand, half hoping that perhaps Bell had stayed late and that maybe they could talk, really talk, she thought of the new house and turned suddenly with a found purpose, walked through the kitchen and out the back door again. She would see it properly. The sun arced down now, a yellow rivulet of heat. The men were dressing themselves and talking in a huddle, they didn't see her as she went, walking steadily toward the barn and then past it without entering the pasture so that she approached the side door of the new house.

Her first thought upon entering was that they could rent the place, she didn't know why she hadn't thought of it before. It was not large, but plenty for a couple or even a smallish family and it was far enough from the big house so that it afforded some privacy. She didn't mind devoting her time to cleaning it, as it would free her from the big house and before long they would take additional income and that would satisfy Orren — if Orren could be satisfied.

The kitchen of the new house was as she remembered it, low-ceilinged and tiled in orange and white. The linoleum floor crackled as she walked across it. The room smelled like the inside of an old drawer and it reminded her fitfully of her uncle's trailer with its close walls and its spent fluorescent lighting always on the dim. Her lips steeled against each other in dislike.

She drew out random drawers and found more cooking utensils that she'd not seen on her first trip. A small closet housed the hot-water heater and an old spinterish mop. In another, only cleaning supplies smelling of ammonia. Down the small hallway, Aloma passed the bathroom with its louvered blinds and ceramic sink bowl striped with yellow stalagmited water stains. Then a door which she knew to be Cash's from the guitar posters. And the last room that could only be Emma's.

She stepped into the dark room, touched

by the anemic light that faltered through the blinds. The bed was unmade. A pair of women's shoes lay at the foot of the bed, one shoe tipped over on its side, its toe toward the door. Aloma stepped into the trapped air, tasted the dust and disuse there, smelled the fading perfume of clothing absent its owner. On the bedside table lay a few bobby pins with their legs crossed, a hairbrush, a tiny New Testament, and a framed photograph of Orren held upside down by his older teenaged brother, who gripped him like an up-ended shoat about the middle. Orren's hair fell straight down from his head, his ridiculous grin was a frown.

She took it up in her hands and turned around to carry it to the window in the hallway where she could see it better, but as she turned she felt rather than heard Orren move into the room. Aloma started and nearly dropped the frame. Then she could not decide if she should return the photo to its bedside post or leave and she wanted to do both. Instead, she walked toward Orren quickly, less from a desire to go to him than to keep him from coming farther into the room.

What are you doing? he said.

She was almost under his chin when she stopped, nerves whisked the moist out of her mouth. Well, she said, I had an idea. Something I want to ask you about.

Looks to me like you come to some kind of decision all by your own self.

No, she said. It's just you all were busy and I didn't —

That ain't your picture.

She looked down at the frame in her hand. Orren, she said, but the words did not follow on his name. He waited, seemed to be coming toward her when he had not moved at all.

Orren, she started again and stepped away from him to put the picture down on a nearby bookshelf so Orren's own young face turned out happily to the small room. I thought we might could rent this place out. Make some money for the farm. You work so hard and —

This is their house, he said.

Well, I know — she said and there was a soft desperation in her voice that even she could hear.

I ain't never asked you to come down here.

You did so, she said louder, trying her best to rein in the anger in her voice, and she meant not the newer house, but the whole of the farm and his life.

This ain't your house, he said again.

I know, Orren, but I live here now.

You don't live *here*, he snapped and he stepped up and grasped her hand hard then and he pulled her roughly toward the hall where a small window faced southwest and he raised a forearm and she saw that the muscles of his arm shook as he did this. You live there, he said and his voice chilled her along the length of her spine. He pointed toward the big house. There, he said again.

She didn't look at the house. She looked at him. Emma and Cash don't live here anymore, Orren, Aloma said. They're dead. A silence divided the air between them and neither of them moved even when they felt its cold. She watched as Orren's eyes changed so that they looked past her, through her to the room she stood in and she hated it the instant she saw it, the emptiness she didn't know but might one day come to know. She preferred a yelling to the apparition of life she saw there now. She wanted to wrench her arm away, but she was cautious, she pulled her arm away from his grasp gently as if he were sleeping and she did not want to wake him. And because she could not bear to see his eyes like that, she walked past him out the door and as she stepped out into the dying day, her shadow cast back toward the building, stretching out interminably until it became just a spear thin enough to break.

She'd kept her temper in her mouth, but her ire was up and rising. Aloma marched straight into the house, up the stairs, tearing off her clothes as she went to stand trembling under the cold shower. She shook there with a kind of stupefied, grieved hate for her life. She did not even soap herself, but watched as the water rinsed the dust of the new house, of the fields, from her arms and legs, from her calloused feet. Then with her face drawn to a bitter point, she dressed in one of her old school tee shirts and a pair of tattered shorts and went back down to the kitchen. She was ready to fight, the tiny bones of her fingers trembled.

But Orren did not come to fight. Aloma wrenched open the door and saw nothing but the heated gloaming, the sun's wake, the great red swaths that spoke of its passage. She had refused to look behind her as she left the little house, so she had not seen where Orren had gone. That he was coming back there was no doubt. But she could not force herself to eat so she sat uselessly in a kitchen lit by a sun that was already gone, her feet aggravating the floor. And yet as the hour slagged toward supper and past and still he had not come in, she allowed herself to imagine for a moment what it might be for him not to come back at all. Her mind fretted around the idea. Then, as a kind of retributive punishment, she permitted herself the memory of the last look on his face before she had walked out.

When the light in the room was finally damped by darkness, Aloma rose and switched on the single naked bulb by the stove. She dumped chicken into grease without flouring it and let it heat to a fry with no intention of eating it, only a vague wish to busy her hands. She stood in the small round of light created by the incandescent bulb. Every evening was like this, the night taking the day with no clear demarcation of its passing so she could not mark the precise moment when night arrived again. It took her continually by surprise and she had grown to hate that.

Aloma left the stove and the sounds of the grease popping and sizzling and stood on the back steps. Even in the full dark, the farthest fields disappeared against the shadow of the mountains, dark as night, darker even. She waited for the uneven signaling of lightning bugs among the plants. The tractor stood in silhouette at the gate nearest the house and she detected the passing flutter of bats above her as they sloped about the eaves. The smell of the frying chicken was warm and yeasty as it moved past her into the clean smell of the outdoors. Beyond the steps, she could smell only the grass and beyond it, perhaps, the first hint of cut plants in their nascent decay. She thought to turn around and return to the yellow light of the kitchen, but she sat where she was, unable to care suddenly if the chicken burnt to a crisp in the oil. She felt the heat behind her and the cooler air before her, and pressed between the two, she could not move. Her hands lay like pale empty baskets on her thighs. She closed her eyes, her back bowed. He would come back, he would come back.

The smell of a cigarette drifted to her. Then she heard Orren approaching from the other side of the house. When he turned the corner of the house and saw her, he paused and then leaned against the house itself, watching her.

Where have you been? she said, low and tight.

Nowhere.

Nowhere . . .

What are you doing? he said.

Waiting.

Aloma, he began.

I've been waiting here for you, she said again, louder.

Orren exhaled roughly through his nose and looked down. Then he drew his left hand out of his pocket and placed it on his hip. But still he did not straighten up.

Don't you have anything to say to me, Orren?

About what, he said to the ground.

About what we were talking about, she pressed.

We ain't renting out no part of this place, he said.

Do you ever listen to me at all? she said and her voice was acid and then her temper surged free. You didn't even bother to come up for supper. You're never here, Orren. It's like you're leaving me without leaving your own damn property.

No, he said.

Well, don't think for a second I believe you're doing this for me. None of this is for me, she said.

He looked up then, but a long breakable moment passed before he said, What's that supposed to mean?

All of this is for them, Orren, and they're not even here. You kill yourself and they're already killed. Why don't you —

Shut up, Aloma, he said.

Don't tell me to shut up, she snapped, ready to fight. But before she could say another word, he turned and slipped around the corner of the house. In an instant, she was up from her seat on the steps and running around the corner after him. She caught up to him as he stalked through one of the squares of light that shone through the windows on the north side of the house. She reached twice for the shirt fabric at his elbow before she found it with her fingers. He wouldn't turn to meet her so she grabbed awkwardly again at his elbow to force him around. And then he did turn and he wrenched her arm up with all the strength of his right hand and struck her own arm so hard against her chest that her teeth rattled in her mouth and she stumbled back a few paces, tripping, groping wildly out at nothing. Orren's face in the yellow streaming light was wild and he raised his hand and it pointed accusation at her, his words all secondary. You, he said, gathering up his words, you spoiled bitch. You're a goddamn spoiled bitch, he said. His voice was higher than was natural, not his own, but inherited from atavic fury. His throat caught and a strangled sound was stoppered there. Aloma secured her ground before him, all eyes, and a hard joy of awaited engagement rose up in her, her blood rose up in her. He came forward one long step. They cut off my legs, Aloma, he said. They cut off my legs and you want me to run.

But what about me! Think about us! she cried.

What about you? You don't know nothing about it, none of it. You got no feeling. All you care about is being happy. I — and he thudded his own chest with the butt of his hand — I can't have that, that ain't a option. You get me? He took a step back and she saw his letheless fury in the full light of the window and the tears that figured on his face. But he came back again, stalking forward as if to grab at her, but stopping short before her so she didn't know if he would hit her or only speak, but he spoke, saying, And leaving. I ain't the one leaving. His finger again, right at her mouth. You, you, you, he said and she found she couldn't turn away even though his hands weren't on her. You, darlin, are the one fixing to leave. I'm just digging deeper in what you think's a empty well, but all the while you're looking out. He cast his hand out toward the outlying dark. You're looking out, Aloma, I ain't stupid. So don't tell me I'm fixing to leave. I never left a thing I loved.

Orren turned on his last word as if to get away without his own sentence touching him, walking out of the cast light of the window so that he became the vague shape of his lighter clothing and then a brisk shadow, then no different from the rest of what Aloma couldn't see. It took her a moment to gather herself up, she panted in the dark as an animal pants, her mouth was dry. She felt her arm would bruise to the bone. She folded its shaking length to her belly and looked desperately around, her eyes wide, her pupils dilated for any small light to be found in the dark.

She came around the side of the house as a sleepwalker might, barely propelled by an expiring rage and stumbling. The air was muggy around her, the heat of the day still expressed in the air. She stepped into the light of the kitchen and smelled the black acrid burning of meat. The chicken was ruined. As she slid the skillet to a cold burner, somber, barely moving, but her heart still beating with a kind of heady unease that made her strangely glad, Orren's accusation came again. Again she heard the word — leaving — and she began to touch the thing, to turn it over and over in her mind like a worry bead.

* * *

He did not come to bed with her. When she awoke, it was to the unapologetic knocking of his boots approaching the room and she knew from the way he stopped at the door and came no farther that he was still angry.

I need you up, he said.

She lay on her side facing the window. For what? she said flatly without turning around, her mouth half sunk in a pillow.

I'm fixing to finish this harvest.

Now she turned around. His face was without expression, but there were purpling circles under his eyes. What about those men you hired? she said.

I let em go yesterday. I can't afford no two days what I can do with you.

But —

Get up, it's late, he said and he took one long stride into the room, reached down and snatched at the sheets so they came off her white naked supine body and she said, Hey, sharply, as if he'd never seen her naked before and yanked the sheets back to cover herself. She glared at him.

Up, he said, no choicing in his words.

Alright, she said in a voice too loud for the room so he turned and left with one hand up like she couldn't be suffered and she sat up straight in the bed, propelled by something akin to hate. She jerked the covers off herself now that he had retreated and she stomped to the closet, but she did not want to ruin any of her clothes so she struggled into one of his long-sleeved shirts and a pair of his jeans and belted them tight. She smelled like him now, as if she were wearing him, and that irritated her, but not as much as the memory of him yanking her sheets away. She glared at the door frame as though he were still standing there and she argued with him in her mind as she walked out the back door and marched down to the half-harvested field.

* * *

They did not talk as they worked. Orren stooped with a knife and he severed a plant below the butt where it strove from the soil, wagering its stalk for the sun. Then he stood and skewered the neck on the holed stick where it would dry before being tied and hung from the high rafters of the black barn. He demonstrated her this once without saying anything and then she bent in the neighboring row and with her own knife struck her first plant above its roots. When it fell, she grasped the thing up and with both hands drove it onto the stake through its sharp silver topper, cutting clean through the strong stalk. There the aborted plant hung and shortly began to wilt and wither against its supports, dying into itself. They worked in a sweating silence along side-by-side rows as though the other were not there. Orren did not look up at her as he worked. All morning he cut and speared, hovering over the plants and his own thoughts, and she followed him as best she could up the rows, but he was much stronger, much quicker, and soon he was moving down her row toward her, bending, spearing, bending, spearing.

Before noon they'd left two windrows of plants to wilt.

When the sun was high and they'd drunk all the water in a gallon jug, she said curtly, Food time, and turned to the house to make sandwiches. She did not want him to see how her arms shook with the morning's efforts. In the first-floor bathroom she saw the sun had burned her cheeks already and she'd sweated through Orren's shirt. She looked even younger than she was, she thought, with high color on her cheeks and her hair platted back, a ragged thing with dislike etched on her sunworn face. She eyed her hurt arm acidly, it had failed to bruise sufficiently.

In the field, Orren ate the three shoddily made sandwiches she handed him, but he did not say thank you, he did not even bother to inspect what he was eating. And she thought him to be like an animal as he ate unthinkingly, she stared at him while he chewed. Her eyes dared him to continue their last night's argument, but he tolerated her only a short time before he turned around and faced to the east. Then she stared mutely at his back. When he had eaten his full, they set to work again. But unlike the morning, she found that the afternoon under the sun sapped her strength. By two the breeze stilled and the heat swelled up like something dead and she felt her skin burning as she sticked and spread the leaves of the plants. When they moved up a row, they faced the mountains away from the sun and her body complied with her mind's bidding to stoop, cut, and spear without pausing. But coming down a row, her mind roamed free in a sun-driven fever from her body, she could think of very little but stopping. Each motion to stoop burned her thighs and a hard fiery line traced up her back. Her hands swelled around the haft, her fingers rusted into their grip. She glanced occasionally at the house as she went, but her laboring mind could no longer stir up any kind of feeling for it, not even resentment. It offered its own kind of shade. She looked across the row at Orren, the way his shoulders scissored as he cut and his sweat soaked his shirt against him. What he did, she saw, was tilt his head down like a man in a heavy wind, so that the sun glanced off him, burning the back of his neck only, while he remained tucked into himself, preserving himself. His hands never ceased their motions. He looked only at the plot of earth before him, nothing else. Aloma tucked her own head without realizing it.

When the afternoon wasted toward evening and still they hadn't spoken a word, she heeled up behind him, half drunk with fatigue, and she kicked out brazenly at his boot so that he turned around and looked up at her, drawing his struck leg under him.

Oh, just say something, she said.

He stared at her, his knife with its sharp lip against the filthy cotton of his pant leg. What? he said.

She groaned and he shrugged. Then she said, I did pretty good work, huh? And he nodded once and went back to cutting. She sighed. She'd worked fast, and for not having known what she was doing, she'd managed the job of a man, bending and stooping until her back was about to break, all without complaining.

I'm hungry. I guess you can clean up, she said. I'm going up to the house.

He narrowed his eyes at her. Alright, I got a cow to check on. She shrugged the way he had and she turned on her heel and left him in the middle of the rows, still kneeling in the dirt and watching her leave him.

But she didn't make him anything. It was unfitting, she knew, but in her fever she felt the sun had leached the very marrow from her bones and Orren himself had somehow caused the sun to rise. So she left him to his own devices and she knew them to be few. She ate bologna and white bread straight out of the refrigerator and when she saw him coming up past the willow, she abandoned the room, still hungry but resolved not to spend another minute in his presence. He could sleep down at the new house for all she cared, he could sleep with the cows.

She was already upstairs and showered before she realized she had not gone down to the church at all today. With all the cutting and spearing she had completely forgotten to play piano for the first time since she'd taken the job. She stood still in her nightgown when she realized it. It disconcerted her, how it all seemed backward. How she'd worked with Orren all day but wanted to be almost anywhere else in the world, maybe most of all on another drive with Bell, and she'd not even realized it until just this moment. She thought again of what Orren had said last night and she felt suddenly a flower of panic bloom across her chest and she wanted not to escape the house so much as she wanted to

241

escape all of it and mostly herself, a self she found to be increasingly shifty and desirous in ways that frightened her when she looked too closely.

But these thoughts vanished when she heard Orren's slow naked footfalls on the wooden stairs and she hurried to the bed and pulled the covers over her. She heard him approach the room. Way down on the road, a car passed and a whiter ghost of light flickered momentarily on the still-lit wall. Aloma followed the glimmer with her eyes and strained for the falling sound of its passage.

Don't come in here if you can't say a decent word, she said when she judged him to be at the door. But he came in anyway and as she had demanded, he did not say a word. He simply undressed and walked down the hallway to the shower and stood under the water for a long time so she wondered if he was going to go on back down to the new house, but when he came out and dried off, he did not go anywhere else but walked to the bed. She sighed loudly. Twice. Then she rolled onto her side and took most of the sheets with her. He sat down on his side of the bed. She sighed again and looked out the window. She squeezed her eyes shut as he lowered himself to stretch full length on the mattress and thought of how she'd push him away if he tried to touch her and she was still thinking of ways to punish him when she fell asleep.

★ ★ ★

It was a far reach to find him, he was much taller than her. She felt his breath near her. One hand slid between her legs, she waited and waited for the weight of him on her mouth, her eyes closed, until she realized she was touching herself in a dream of her own making. And when she knew it to be Bell's face in her mind, her eyes darted open and she gasped out loud. Orren awoke to the sound of her intaken breath, his head rising from the pillow.

What? he said, confused.

She looked at him in fear for a moment, frightened that he would see the dream written on her like so many words. Then, without thinking, she wound herself around him and pulled at his mouth with her own and found him with her hand and he was hard in an instant and inside of her the next. She said his name over and over, concentrating with all her might, as if to reassure herself that it was Orren she wanted and hoping to call her own name out of him until every word he possessed would rise up and spill over her. But no words came. So she scratched at him and grabbed at him until she was striking him, but no matter what she did, he was silent as the grave as he fucked her.

★　★　★

Aloma could not rise the next morning. When the dawn insinuated its bluing white light into the room, she could not face it and so veiled her eyes with the sheet. She told Orren she was ill and he went down to make his own coffee and his own paltry breakfast. She waited for the final sound of the back door opening and closing and in her mind she configured him walking, the sun weaving a living red into the brown of his hair as he walked alone to his work. Aloma moved her legs under the sheet and they resisted her, the enervated muscles hot to the touch and weak. They did not feel like her own. She could not remember ever being so tired, and though her body ached from the cutting, she felt that it was not due only to the work she had done, but that some greater burden was upon her. Her dream hung over in her veins like a liquor, it accused her now in the bald daylight. She screwed her eyes shut. She thought of her small room at the school and how much she had wanted to leave, how she had lain like this and scried her future on the backs of her own eyelids as though they were a crystal ball. She remembered too the black yawn of the driftmouth near her uncle's trailer, its loose rock like broken teeth, its interior a black shaft to nowhere. She had once been dry-mouthed for the unimpeded morning light beyond the steep holler walls and here she was, on her side under white sheets the open sun lit brilliantly like the sides of a tent in the free light of morning, and still she wanted something, still she was unsatisfied. When had she ever once been full? So that she would not have to answer such an inquiry from herself, she forced her mind back to sleep.

But she woke to herself and she stumbled sore and disoriented from the bed, her mind still cleaving to sleep. She knew only that she could remain no longer in their bed and the same galloping unease that drove her from the bed drove her from the house itself. She did not go to the back door first to search for Orren and she did not make him any food or even go down to the barn to check the chickens she had already neglected in the early hours of the morning. She simply picked up her keys and left without asking herself where she was going or why.

She drove across the county into Hansonville and her half-lid eyes undressed the place as she passed, her face sober. The whole of it was small, graceless. There was not a building in the town that was more than two stories high. She parked out front of the church, looking north to where the county ended, where the road ran on and on. Then she scrabbled through the scores she kept on the passenger-side seat, but in the end grabbed one randomly, anything would suit. She would go inside and play on the piano because she could not think what else to do. And she would make noise, the box would resonate with sound only because it was empty, it did nothing of its own accord, it only waited for her to make it sing.

Aloma brought a hand to her brow and peered through the gate of her fingers to clear her thoughts. Was it only that she was tired of herself today? Or was it that every time she sat down before a piano now she heard in it, in the falling keys, a metronomic ticking that announced the hours that she did not know how to fill because she did not know if she was coming or going. Or who she would come or go with. She shook her head and opened her eyes, and taking up her score, she walked inside.

★ ★ ★

She had barely spread her fingers on the keys when Bell appeared in the doorway and said, Aloma, I need you in the office.

Of course, she said. She rose from the piano, the last strings still vibrating behind her, and followed him out of the little sanctuary. Bell was seated again at the desk in his office when she paused in the doorway. His black Bible was closed and pushed against the wall.

Set down a minute, he said and she sat with her hands in her lap and looked at his face, which had always struck her as a pleasing face but she now thought held some new veiling she'd never noticed before. That surprised her.

He turned to her, he did not smile.

Aloma, he said, I need your home address.

For a moment she did not breathe. What for? she said.

I'm fixing to change the way I pay you. I'm sending it out now instead of just handing it to you.

Oh, she said, looking from one side of the small office to the other, then at the plywood door, but not at him. Oh, that's not necessary. I'm fine just to take it the old way.

I need your address, Miss Aloma, he said

247

and the way he called her miss drew her eyes to him. His face was quiet, the pen in his hand did not move but was suspended point-down over a sheet of paper. She could think of no lie, so she said, Fourteen Burnt Ridge Road.

He laid his pen down. He laid it down so softly that it frightened Aloma and she did not dare to move. He nodded.

You are living with Orpheus up at the Fenton place, he said. When she said nothing but only sat there with her lips parted and her breathing uneven, he said, Are you married to him? She shook her head slowly. She watched the expression on his face alter in a way she could not read, then his eyes cut away. How come you didn't tell me you were with this man?

When she spoke, her words rustled out in a whisper. I thought you wouldn't want to hire me to play in your church.

That's right, he said quickly. I would not have. That may sound unchristian, but I would not have. I can't abide that kind of deceit.

But it's not deceit to —

He cut her off with one raised calloused hand. It's deceit to play married when you're not. Quit fooling yourself. And quit trying to fool me.

He tilted his head down then to contain his expression so that she could only see the top of his black curls. He stayed like that with his head bowed, but for how long she did not know and she could not remember later, because when he raised his head he was angry and she had never seen that before.

You deliberately misled me, he said. You just walk into my church here — our church — and live a lie with us, saying you're not attached to a man. But you are very much attached to a man. You may not be married, but you are bound for better or worse whether you know it or you don't. For now and forever since you done it. I don't know what you thought you were doing here . . . His dark eyes slashed at her. I don't know what — But he did not finish his thought, only dampered the sentence while it was still burning in his throat. But still something was rising up in him and she felt it coming and winced even before he spoke it.

You are foolish, he said. You are pretty, you play pretty music, but you are foolish. He stopped suddenly and he brought his hands together and bowed his forehead again atop the box of his two hands. Aloma did not think then to defend herself, she had no defense. She just watched him, watched him without blinking, waiting.

With his head still down, he said, Aloma, don't grant yourself permission to be ungodly just because you're young. Maybe you think it's some small thing to stir up love, but you're wrong. And then he said nothing more. When he lifted his head finally and their eyes met, Aloma looked away, pale.

I'll go, she said quietly, finding her voice, surprised that it didn't tremble. She drew her feet firmly under her, ready to rise.

Yes. Go, he said. I want you to go.

She stood up and moved to the door. Then she turned and said, Who told you?

Mother, he said. Mrs. Breathitt told her.

Who's that? said Aloma.

She owns the grocery down near your place.

Aloma almost laughed. Then she turned to go, but did not leave before he said her name one more time, saying, I owe you money. But she just said, No, no, you don't, and could not find it in her to look back.

★ ★ ★

She sat in the stillness of her truck for a long time, willing herself to move, afraid Bell would come out and yet unable to turn the key, staring straight ahead, her breathing coming hard and fast. Why was it still light?

250

She wished the day would go. She fidgeted with the sunbleached wheel, with the knob of the stick, her hands ran in repeating swipes down the denim over her thighs, she could not stop. Her empty hands had stolen something. The knowledge cut her with a guilt that was so clear and so sudden, she didn't know how she'd not felt its sharp edge before, her own feeling numbed by some dulling desire. She couldn't name the thing she'd stolen, she could not hold it in her hand, though she could break it to bits, and she didn't know whether it belonged to Orren or Bell or both, she only knew that she had done it. And she knew because the guilt that came was clear as a road sign pointing her back to the house. She turned the ignition suddenly and gunned once, drove home in a heat, forgetting her scores on the piano and not remembering them until much later. She thought to cry, but she would not grant herself the comfort of easy remorse and the wind whipped her eyes dry, relentless. She passed through the land without seeing it, finding her way home by an old habit newly felt.

When she came to the house, when it appeared from a distance almost gray because of the paint stripping away from the weathered boards, she found the sight of it, even its ugliness, not beautiful — it could never be that — but bearable in its unremarkable way. And better, far better, than a roving desire that searched the horizon for new locations in which to discover an easier love, as if love — mixed and diluted with laziness — could still be love. Bell's words lashed her, she shivered with shame. She shaded her eyes with one hand as she drove up the long gravel drive. The sun was already leading west. The days, without her noticing, had grown short.

Orren's truck was parked before the porch and she traced a desperate full circle around the house, though she was half afraid to face him. Still, she sought after him. He was not in the shorn fields or in the curing barn where the first cuts of gathered tobacco now hung drying from the rafters. She did not see him down in the pasture or in the doorway to the barn, though she saw chickens scratching at the dirt in the foreyard. The door to the new house was not open. Aloma turned and looked directly at the sun then, as if she would find him there, but she could only close her eyes to its fierce ebullience. She realized that for once the night would be cool.

With nothing else to do, Aloma went into the kitchen and cooked. After an hour, there was still no sign of him. So she sat at the small table in the kitchen, though she could not bring herself to eat, listening for sounds of him. Birds passed overhead and called for the end of summer, then were gone. The noise of the day stilled into reverend silence and darkness fell. When she stood up finally from the kitchen table and peered out the back door and thought of wandering into the fields to find him, it was full black. The tobacco banked in shadow under the cold wink of Venus. Perhaps when all was said and done, Orren did not want her to find him. Her mind twisted around this new thought.

She went upstairs and sat on the bed in her clothes, but she did not lie down. She studied the dark room about her. Her mind strove for a place to rest, but could not settle. The lonesomest thing she knew, her childhood, rose before her like a shade, but she shooed it away with a blink of her dark-accustomed eyes. Her mind veered away from Bell and the shame that instantly burned her face and it tried to veer away from Orren too, who, she saw now with a clarity brought on by defeat, she had fought not to love even as she had asked him for love. But who had there been to teach her otherwise? As a lone girl growing into adulthood, she had only her own body to touch, her restless mind curbed by the borders of her own imagination. She'd never known the burden or the joy of contouring herself to another. She had only ever had herself. And when Orren came, love was only an accident, her spirit carried into the thing through the strivings of her body, her heart surprised suddenly to find itself a mortise. Bell was right, she was tenoned to Orren. And once the thing was done, it was too late to consider how they loved across a distance of three counties and two mountains, or that once the distance was crossed, distance would still remain. Aloma peered hard into the dark suddenly, thinking what a waste it was to ever think of going, how wasteful — not ungodly, as Bell had said, but wasteful of creation, which maybe was the same thing — to run and seek after another only to find that the gulf was there too, built into creation as one found it, bred into the act of love. And she did not know what to do with that, or how to reconcile any of it. She only knew that she had indeed been foolish, for thinking that the easy thing was the one worth wanting.

Then she heard her name being called and she could not tell where it was coming from, a revenant call from the house itself. When it came again, she rushed sightless into Orren and Cash's old room, pushed up a window, and peered out into the indigoed land. This time her name sounded clearly across the distance and she saw a moving shape, Orren, barely visible as a shadow amidst the uneven shadows of the pasture. He waved his arm or seemed to, and without hesitating, she raced from the room and down the steps to the back door in her slippers, her heart rising as he called her name again. She stumbled down the hill toward him. Orren came up out of the pasture and met her halfway on the incline.

I need you, he said.

I didn't know where you were, she said.

I got a cow that's calving.

What? Why didn't you tell me?

He raised his hands up in a useless gesture.

Orren, you never tell me anything, she said.

I can't see how it's coming, he said. Fetch me that flashlight from the kitchen — and when she turned toward the house, which she did instantly because of the need in his voice — he said, And a blanket too. Get a blanket and come back down here quick. She ran back into the house again and up the steps to the second floor. She yanked a woolen comfort from their bed and then she retraced her way out into the dark, quick but ginger, for she could see nothing. She found Orren kneeling beside the cow on the far side of the barn on a grassy patch of earth that had not been muddied by hooves. The cow had already lain down of her own volition without tying, her ribs carved meanly as she breathed, waxing gaunt as she inhaled, smoothing into her flesh again as the air passed through her open mouth and nostrils.

What I don't know is if she calved ever . . . said Orren when he saw Aloma turn the corner with the comfort and flashlight in her hands. I don't know how old she is, he said and ran his hands through his hair and then down across his knees, and with his naked arms, which he had scrubbed till his skin chafed in the kitchen sink, he reached into the cow. Into the wet warm birth canal, scooting forward, he reached farther into that pressing dark and said, Wait.

What?

That don't pencil.

What?

Legs, but no head. Is it reared? But it don't feel right. He spoke more to himself than to her. He pulled his hand out and looked down at the cow on her side, her barrel chest rising and falling rapidly, and then looked down at his own hand to cipher on his flesh what he had felt. Shine that light, he said, though it did little but show up the mucus and wet on his skin as he returned his arm into the rubied folds of the cow. She's teeny, he said and with his arm still in her, he peered over his shoulder at Aloma and said, Now, that's why I ain't still got that bull here, see. She's little — and he turned again to face the birthing — but what the hell is . . . Then he said, Oh goddamn, its neck is crooked back is what.

And she said, Should we call the vet? but Orren said nothing, all the force of his eyes and arms working to follow the steep curve of the calf's grudging neck to its jaw, to pull it toward his own body and the brisk night air. Aloma saw he was sweating despite the cold. A contraction wrenched his arms against the implacable bones guarding the baby and Orren cried out softly twice.

Orren, should I call him? Aloma hoped toward it with her voice. The flashlight shone a yellow hoop on the ground between Orren's muddied knees. He did not answer immediately, though he stopped the wrestling of his hand in the womb, feeling only the heavy, inert, perhaps already dead calf under his fingers. He said, Fifteen minutes.

That's too long, she said, scared, though she did not really know.

No, it's short. Shit, I don't know, he said and he groped farther for the jaw. But the contraction caught him and he said, No, goddamn it, no no no, and he reached with the feeble remaining strength of his arm clamped in her spasm. The cow bawled like a living horn and Aloma cried, Orren, please!

No, he said sharp and she fell back a step, the hoop of light expanded so she saw all the muscles of his body gathered up in pure will. She said nothing further. The silence was broken only by the heavy breathing of the cow and the bawling that erupted from her as if in surprise or in anger. The night air was cool and the cow's breath bloomed in the chilled air each time she exhaled. Grayed wisps like smoke rose from her damp hide. Aloma draped the comfort over her own shoulders as Orren knelt and pressed and turned and pushed at the calf's submerged shape until finally the stubborn head came forefront and then with his own face nearly at the cow's anus, Orren reached and found both legs.

Now, he said, and as if in answer, the cow pushed and then the hooves came like two iron pokers and Orren tore away the sac that surrounded them. He made a chuffing sound like laughing, but it was only a small gasping after victory and then the nose of the calf, raw and heavy with mucus, protruded. Aloma gaped.

Come now, he said and it came, but slowly. Come, he said and it inched a bit more until the head swelled out suddenly like a bloodied balloon from the birth canal and Aloma gripped hard the flashlight for fear she would drop it. Here it was. Now Orren grasped the wetted fetlocks, pulled one leg and then the other as he tried to walk the shoulders out and Aloma could not even blink as she watched the calf come. Orren said, Push push push, but it was not enough, the calf was too big, his new life could not break free of her grasp on him, so that Orren had to lean back, using all the force of his own body, and he pulled at the protruding calf like a starving man pulling a sack of grain until it passed finally through, sliding quickly at the last, out of the mother and into the night.

God, said Aloma, the light shaking in her hands. Orren swiped the blood and mucus from the calf's squared mouth and nostrils and tickled up one nostril and blew in that nostril and then the other and when that did nothing, nothing at all, he slapped its broadside with the flat plate of his hand. The calf hauled air and Orren pattered his hands down the sodden hide, thumping and kneading and to get away from this unmothering, the calf moved, struggling up on its strange new legs, first placing weight on its pasterns, its nose pushing up and up as if it were pressing against a great and horrible weight, and then with another burst, it rose up on its legs, all four. It swayed forward and back, then to the side and just as Aloma reached out to keep it from tumbling over onto its flank — ignoring Orren as he shook his head to keep her — the calf jerked awkwardly to one side, caught its own weight and then, with the motions of a groggy stilted bird, righted itself. All the while, the cow lay on her side, her reedy breaths accompanied the first steps of her calf. She lifted her head to find the calf in the dark and bawled a sound that caused the hair on Aloma's neck to stand up. The cow made a jerking attempt to rise, but did not. Then the air in her lungs whistled through her nose narrowly. Orren seemed to have forgotten her for a moment as he watched the calf, his own face gleaming with sweat, his hair damp. He had knocked his cap off long ago and it lay behind him, ground into the mud. He rocked on his haunches and watched the calf stumble and jolt forward a few paces and then, finding its newborn rhythm, it stepped away from their inner circle. Aloma still held the flashlight in her hands, the beam trained on the ground. She clicked it off and for a moment they remained in the early-morning dark together with the uneven gasping of the mother.

Orren roused himself suddenly and said, Rub the calf down with that blanket. She did as she was told, she bent down and enfolded it in her arms, felt the lath-thin ribs of the calf as she did so, half afraid of its newness. It shook, but did not resist her, it nuzzled repeatedly at her shoulder and when it found no teat, it gazed straight ahead into the cold dark with its enormous black eyes. Behind them, Orren scrambled around the bulk of the cow and knelt at her head, whispered something to her under her own breathing, something only she could hear, and then he pulled firmly at her head with both hands and when she moaned but did not rise, he passed his hands over her hind legs, prodding.

No good, said Orren.

What is it?

She can't raise up.

What?

It got a nerve. It can paralyze them. That calf was a long time coming and it was big too. I think she's bleeding.

Orren reached inside the cow again, feeling along the uterine walls.

What are we gonna do? Aloma said, still bent in her awkward embrace of the calf.

Oh shit, he said. She's tore. His slippery fingers clamped together the sides of the tear, but after some minutes the blood continued to pass and would not thicken. With nothing left to do, Orren pulled his hand from the womb and stood up, breathing hard. He stared down at the blood on his hand. Aloma watched him, but said nothing.

Set for a bit, Orren said suddenly. I'm gonna heat a bottle. Keep that calf warm. Then he jogged back up toward the house, leaving Aloma with the animals. The mother breathed, the calf breathed. Aloma knelt beside the calf, using the ends of the blanket to gentle it, patting its new hide dry. She looked up at the sky, craning her neck until she had stretched herself a straight line from her clavicle to her chin. Venus was unleashed, pure white, but she could not see Orion, he was obscured by the fall of the land. When the calf bawled once, she heard the other cows answer softly from under the gallery.

When Orren returned, he brought with him a rifle and a two-quart bottle. He knelt before the calf, the rifle behind him, and fed the calf straight from the bottle, patting its nose, patting its flanks. They said nothing for a while as the calf drank and butted against Orren's hand. Then he passed the emptied bottle to Aloma and moved to the cow, knelt for a time by her legs again. When he finally stood from his long crouch, his own legs were unsteady from being tucked under him and he caught himself against the fencing at the side of the barn to keep from stumbling.

Orren, Aloma said.

He shook his head.

Don't, she said.

She done good. It's a hour on. I can't a known, he said and he turned toward the prone bulk of the cow again. I waited too long. He rubbed at his face with one dirty hand. I can't a known if she calved ever. Cassius done it all, Cassius always known what to do. You think somebody could a told me something. Nobody ever learned me to do it alone. He looked at Aloma then with his expression unraveling for a moment before he stepped over the cow's legs and reached for his rifle.

Go on up at the house if you want, he said. She just stared at him as he loaded the cartridge into the chamber of his rifle and threw the bolt. When he saw that she was not leaving, Orren said, Set back and cover up the ears on that calf. And your own if you're able. He waited a second while she bent and clapped her hands over the large tufted ears of the calf and then he brought the rifle to his shoulder and shot the mother high between the ears.

The sharp crack frightened the calf and it bolted from Aloma's hands, fell down on its forelegs shedding the comfort, and for a few seconds just stayed there, shaking, with its eyes wide. But then it found its feet again and stumbled a few steps, slowed suddenly, and seemed to calm when the sound did not repeat. The unsteady press of its small hooves on the wetted earth was the only sound as Orren lowered the rifle and bent over the cow. She breathed once and died as he bent. Then Aloma heard a rude wail behind her, a sound to shatter leaves, but when she turned her head and there was nothing there, she realized that she'd made the sound herself. She touched a hand to her mouth in surprise, but the sound kept coming so she stifled it with her palm. Her body began to cry, but without tears, hard so she could not breathe. She closed her eyes and she could not see anything, her hand pressed farther into her gaping mouth and without thinking, she began to falter, to sink to a sitting position down onto the churned dirt. But Orren crossed the distance between them. He took her arm, he said, Come on now. I ought not to a let you stay down here. She smelled his sweat and the burnt firecracker smell of the rifle.

She shook her head and he led her forward with an arm around her waist to keep her from stumbling. She seemed unable to open her eyes. Out of the field and across the newly dewed grasses that led to the house. Up the back steps and into the kitchen where he laid the rifle on the counter with a clatter and led her farther into the warm house, up the creaking wooden stairs and into the bedroom. She knew she smelled of manure and dirt, but she was too tired to think and she sat down on the bed like a loose-limbed child and let Orren take off her ruined slippers. Then he undid the button and zipper of her jeans so she could breathe and he pressed her down onto the mattress. Her dry crying subsided. He sat himself and slipped his hand under hers on the mattress and patted out a small music on her knuckles with his thumb. His hand was dry and she felt the dirt caked on his skin. He sat there with her like that for a few minutes and then he said, I'm fixing to go back down there and set with that calf a while. Take care of things. Are you gonna be alright if I leave you here? Or are you fixing to throw yourself out the window? Should I nail it shut first? He made a move as if he was going to do it and she caught him by the filthy-now waistband of his jeans and laughed and her nose ran.

God almighty, he said and he wiped at the snot with the back of his hand. She could smell the musked scent of the cow on his skin. He patted her head once and then she felt the mattress spring up as his weight lifted and he left the room. She lay there for a while, feeling herself being talked down by the quiet of the room and the warmth his hand had transferred and left, briefly, on her hair. Her breathing slowed, hiccupping and faltering its way into evenness and then she slept.

★ ★ ★

When she woke, the sun was strong and she knew it was midmorning. Aloma turned her head and found the high light, confused for a minute as to why she had slept through its rising and why the day had pressed on without her. Then she remembered the cow. Orren was not in bed beside her. She sat up in confusion. Behind her, the sheets on the bed were stained with earth where she had lain, all in the shape of her. With her mind still fragile and fogged, she changed into clean jeans and a tee shirt that belonged to Orren and went downstairs. The coffee was still hot. Aloma poured a cup and then opened the back door and spied Orren down in the cow pasture, bent at the waist over the newborn calf, but she could not determine what he was doing. She slipped her feet into a pair of his work boots, which were far too big for her, and clomped down the sloping

266

hillside until she stood at the board fence.

What's that you're doing? she said to Orren's curved back. He started a bit and turned around, all the while holding a hobbing bottle to the calf's mouth and when he turned, he was smiling. The lines at his eyes rayed down onto his cheeks and she saw the color of his eyes very clearly, their depths irrupted the way sun strikes and illuminates water of considerable depth, and the shot of blue startled her and pleased her. The look of him made her laugh out loud.

Wrestling, he said, smiling, and she laughed again and it was an airy, just-woken sound. Then she quieted and said, Where's the cow? and he said, I got Jack Talbridge to come out with his dead wagon. She's took care of. She's gone. And he turned again to the calf, whose face tilted up for Orren's mothering.

Watch this, he said and he struggled the bottle out of the calf's mouth and took a few fast paces backward and the calf rushed forward, stiff-legged and maniacally reaching for the nipple and Orren tossed back his head and laughed so hard his fresh cap fell off his head. By all rights he should look like hell, Aloma thought. He'd taken a two-day harvest, he'd midwifed this calf, not slept at all last night and yet here he was, better than daylight. She shook her head.

Do it again, she said and he complied and the calf did its little trick of need, but she was not watching the calf.

You're all smiles, she said.

He looked at her, squinting in the morning sun. I'll be all smiles tonight, dear, he sang in a rising voice, I'll be all smiles tonight. Though my heart may break tomorrow, I'll be all smiles tonight.

She shook her head again. Heaven help that voice, she said and took a sip of her coffee. He checked her face with a glance and then he stuck the bottle in the back of his pants and came at the fence, vaulting it with one foot on the second board. Aloma screeched, tried to turn and run and said, No, I've got coffee, but he took it from her hand and tossed it to the ground, coffee spilling black onto the pale mud and the chipped cup landing on its side and he grabbed her, lifted her up against his chest. No, she demanded, but she was already being worked over his shoulder like a feed sack. You smell like shit, she said and struck against his back with her fist. You smell like cow shit, she said again into his shirt and then gave up and let him carry her slack weight. At the steps, he dropped her to her feet and staggered for a moment to catch his breath. They God, he said, his face red. He bent over at the waist and wheezed. They God, woman. She went to strike at his shoulder, but then he stood up abruptly, so that he stood over her and her hand raised up with him, still on his shoulder.

Aloma, I want you should marry me, he said.

She blinked at him, blinked as though the sun were now in her eyes.

Let's get married, he said.

When? she said slowly.

Today.

What?

Marry me today.

She laughed and then sobered. Her eyes narrowed.

We've been about to kill each other, she said and looked down, remembering yesterday suddenly, thinking of Bell's words.

That don't make no difference. You can kill me when we're married.

But things aren't exactly in order, she said and looked out over the land, the pulled cones of drying tobacco that lined the fields and still more fields lying fallow. Isn't that what you've been waiting for all along? Orren followed her gaze outward. The late-morning sun was shortening shadows all over the yard. They stood in the shadow of the house, but it was declining also.

No, things ain't so much in order, you're right.

Well, she said.

But, he said, I've not had a right understanding.

Of what? she said, suspicious.

Of all of it, he said. How it comes and goes.

They stared at each other. Then he shut his eyes as if he'd grown so sleepy he couldn't hold the weight of his eyelids and he said, I don't know how come it is I got to do everything so alone. I'm tired. But it is what it is.

Orren, getting married's not going to make you not alone, she said. And I've been right here the whole time.

I'm alone so long as you got one foot half out the door, he said.

Oh, she said slowly, I see. And she did. Her arm was still raised, her hand still on his shoulder. She slid her fingers up farther and rubbed at his neck and he let her do this for a minute. He opened his eyes. Blue still.

Alright, she said.

He smiled. He leaned down and kissed her on the forehead and they stayed like that until Aloma could feel the heat of his body mingled with the heat of the day, though it was not yet touching them, sheltered in shadow as they were. She listened to him inhaling and exhaling and when she closed her eyes, she saw again the cap falling from his head and his face tilted up and his open mouth like that. She wanted to keep her eyes shut and hold him there in the amber of her mind's eye. But he straightened up and said, How about you call the preacher down at the church and see if maybe he'd do it today.

Oh, she pulled away and tucked her hands in her pockets. Oh. I don't know.

Why not? he said.

She placed a finger up against the inner corner of her eye and wiggled it while she sought out a reason. She screwed up her face. Oh shit, Orren, I don't think he was going in today. I'm not sure.

But he knows my people, said Orren. And then she apprehended in advance what he was going to say so it was almost as if she had scripted the words herself — why had she not realized it before now? He said, He preached over the funerals, and her heart cramped with his words, but she was not surprised, not really. A grief settled onto her breast and it tugged at her so heavily she wanted nothing more than to sink down to the grass and sit in order to bear its weight.

I see, she said again. You sure you don't want to call him? she said hopelessly.

Why don't you, he said and it was settled,

because it was not a question. It was Orren getting his way. Then he enfolded her in his arms so that she could hardly breathe. He kissed her on the mouth this time and looked into her eyes for a moment and she smelled the sweat of the long night on him and she found it difficult to hold his gaze. Then he went upstairs to shower.

Aloma remained in the dark patch on the grass. All the spirit had fled from her now. She turned the thing over in her mind and was sickened by it. So strong was the feeling that she turned and faced the house, gripping her belly, afraid she would be ill standing there. She looked up to the sky as if her salvation was there, but it was not. It never was, she thought bitterly. It was not there the day she said, Yes, yes, I'll come, it wasn't in the cold pasture last night, it wasn't in the car when the sheet metal arced and opened the windshield so that it rained glass. It was not up or down, it was not in a location. It just wasn't like that. The sky above looked to her now like the palm of a great empty hand, never moving any closer, never touching the earth. She sighed.

When she moved, it was as though her body had lost any sense of its own animation. Her footfalls were heavy from the kitchen to the dining room. She picked up the receiver and held it to her ear. She dialed his home number. It rang six times, and she was stabbed with relief that he was not there, but then the line buzzed and she heard his voice.

Hello?

Hello, she said. And because he did not say anything further, she knew he recognized her voice. But when she went to speak, she could not find any words. Finally he said, What is it, Aloma?

I —

Are you calling because you left your books?

What? No, she said, her mind fumbled for his meaning. No. I hate to . . . I have to ask you a favor.

I don't suspect I'm of a mind to do you any favors, Aloma, he said.

She swallowed that and nodded as if he were in the room with her. Yes, she said. Yes, but Orren —

Whatsoever you're fixing to say won't concern me, Bell said.

He only wants you to marry us, she said finally in a queasy rush. I'm so sorry —

Long silence followed by a sigh as he saw the whole of the thing, took the weight and measure of it.

I'm sorry, she added, further chastened by his quiet. He only wants you. He only — And then, choking on her own mortification, Aloma screwed up her face and with a hushed cry, said, Never mind, never mind, I'm sorry, and then let the receiver clatter back into its black hard cradle. Then she covered her ears with her hands to block out the rest of the conversation they didn't have.

Not a minute later the phone rang. She jumped and snatched it up, her heart dreadful.

I will marry the two of you, he said.

She put one hand over her breast. Bell, I know you're not happy —

No, I'm not happy, and frankly, I wish I'd not have to do it. But this ain't about happiness — not mine, nor yours, nor Orren's. If he wants me to do it, I will consent to it. She nodded her head without a word.

I'll be at the church at two tomorrow, he said. Don't make me wait.

★ ★ ★

She wore the prettiest dress she owned, which was old and tight in the bust now, a hand-me-down from a girl at school, but there was no time to find anything that fit well and the rest of her dresses were too plain. Orren wore a brown suit that had been his brother's, a Sunday suit he'd found down in one of the closets in the new house. He didn't know how to tie the tie and neither did she so he left it undone, silken on the bed. As he drove, she sat beside him with the wind blowing her hair so she was mussed and hot and able to busy herself with it to hide her growing trepidation. Then she gave up and closed her eyes for the rest of the drive, her lips pressed tight together, and Orren looked over at her as he drove and at one point he said, You got second thoughts now? And she just looked at him and shook her head, but she could not even pretend to smile and her stomach rolled in on itself like the nighttime leaf of a prayer plant.

The church door was open wide when they arrived and, at the sound of their truck pulling into the gravel of the drive, Bell stepped outside. He stood on the top step and seemed as though he did not notice them, but instead looked out toward the road where there was no passing traffic. He held a small black Bible in one hand, which he pressed to the belt buckle of his pants and his eyes squinted against the sun, but he did not bother to shade his face with his hand. When they left the truck, Aloma trailed behind, but when Bell turned his eyes their way, there was little to be read there. He looked at Orren, not at her. Aloma bowed her head.

Bell reached out and grasped Orren's hand. Orren, he said, I wish Emma was here today. Your father and brother too.

Orren nodded his head.

Aloma, Bell said and there was a hint of chill in his greeting so that when he turned into the church abruptly, it gave Orren pause. He looked at Aloma and then at Bell's retreating back and ran his hand through his hair once before he walked slowly down the aisle. Aloma tried to look at no one at all as she followed.

A man in grass-stained work pants and boots sat in the first pew and turned when he heard them enter. He rose, his black hair falling across his lined forehead, and as he stepped toward the aisle, bits of grass fell from his boots and the legs of his pants, scattering like tiny leaves around a tree.

This is my cousin Saunder, said Bell and he placed a hand on the man's shoulder. He was here cutting the grass. He'll make for a witness today.

Orren shook his hand and Bell stepped onto the first step of the landing and put his own head down for a moment while Aloma and Orren arranged themselves before him and waited. The man beside them smelled faintly of the outdoors. Aloma did not want to look at Bell, her eyes fought it, but she could look nowhere else, she stared up at him. Orren did the same. Then Bell raised his head and called them dearly beloved and he married Orren and Aloma. They had no rings to exchange, only a kiss. So they kissed and then Bell prayed and when he closed his prayer in his coarse voice, he said, Lord, we ask your blessings on these two for they've seen trouble and they have a ways to go yet. They've known suffering, but we are told that whosoever is still among us has his fair share of hope. Lord, help these two live moderate, help them not spend their love on foolishness, not palter away their savings. We ask that your grace be on them. Aloma felt Orren stir beside her then and she opened her eyes to find him staring at Bell and Bell was already looking at them with his own eyes open, so that as Bell finished his prayer they did not appear to be praying at all, but only listening as he said, And it's also written for you to enjoy a simple life with the wife whom you love, for we know that all the days of this worried life, they are everlasting vanity, but they are our given portion, it's written, they hold our labor under the sun, and know that whatsoever your hands find to do, do it with all your might, for in heaven there's no labor at all, but also no wife and maybe no thought, but only the perfect everlasting. And they could not tell then if he was talking to God or Orren or only to himself and then he raised his hands and said, Amen.

When they signed their names to the paper, Aloma found a kind of relief, but it was a milder thing than she'd expected, it did not announce some great shift within her. Orren shook Bell's hand again, as well as the hand of the man who had scattered the bits of grass beneath their feet and smelled of the outdoors. Then they walked down the aisle together toward the daylight beyond the church. But Bell said, Aloma, and they turned, Aloma taking one step toward him with her hand slightly raised as if to silence him, but he went no further. He only held her scores in his hand and said, You left these here. He did not smile and his eyes slashed into hers, but only briefly, before he said, Goodbye, and lifted his hand to them in a way that was easier than he felt and he turned so that he would not see them walk from the church. When she turned, Orren was standing solitary in the aisle, his brows drawn. Aloma grasped up his hand purposefully, the way a mother takes her son's hand, and they walked out of the white church together. Then when she sat in the cab of the truck, she opened her scores and found the cash that Bell owed her tucked between two pages of a song.

★ ★ ★

Orren gripped the wheel with one hand, undid the first pearled buttons of his shirt. The wind from the window ruffled his hair at the crown where it was thinning. He flexed his wheel hand so the topography of his veins and tendons raised up, receded.

He seems like a good man, he said, looking not to either side.

Who — Bell? Aloma said.

Yeah. He nodded and they passed into silence, watching the road.

Halfway home, Aloma said, I quit my job there.

What? When?

Well, only just two days ago, she said.

He looked at her carefully, his foot rising up off the gas just barely. You ain't said a thing about it.

Well, I just kinda up and did it, she said, turning to the window so the wind whipped her mouth and snatched her words away.

And how come is that?

She shrugged and tried her best to look unconcerned as she gazed out. I think I have enough money saved now to rent a piano and

279

I might could teach lessons up at the house. I'll make us some money that way.

He nodded. That seems to me a good idea, Aloma. Then he said, I like to have you around. You think I don't notice when you're up there, but I do. I hear you singing. She looked over at him and watched him inhale deeply and stretch his shoulders and he knew she was watching, but he didn't turn. When he reached into his breast pocket for a cigarette, she took it from his hand and found a lighter in the ashtray, lit it for him, dragged once, and passed it back. Thank you, he said and smoked as Aloma leaned her head way back on the seat so that she could feel the glass jittering in its frame under her head and her teeth rattled just so. Out of the corner of her eye, Aloma watched Orren drive, relieved that he said nothing more. When he turned into the gravel drive, she thought, Here I come back a married woman, but the thought was only a faint breeze, it stirred up nothing new. She looked at herself in the passenger mirror and the sun striking the glass also struck her eyes so they teared and blinked. When her eyes eased up, the truck was stopped and Orren — his cigarette flicked out the window and smoldering still in the gravel — was looking at her.

I got to ask you, Aloma.

What? she said, terrified, for she knew what he would say.

Do you got feelings for that man? He gripped the steering wheel now with both hands. Don't lie to me. I know sometimes you lie to me.

I don't lie to you, she said, genuinely startled.

He shook his head. You think you're not lying to me when you don't say nothing. But you are.

She could not say anything in return, because this was true.

Do you got feelings for that man? Orren said again.

I thought I did, for a while, she said very quietly.

He nodded and looked out over his hands through the windshield glass, up the swell of the yard to the house. She was afraid to follow his gaze, afraid to look anywhere but at his face.

Well, then how come you married me? He said this low, as if he were speaking only to himself.

She thought that over for a minute, not because she wanted to give him a good answer, only one that was no parts lie.

Mostly because I want you.

Like how, you want to fuck me?

Good Lord, Orren, she said and laughed soberly, looking out the side window at the world that was now turning and reddening with force. The change there surprised her eyes. She rubbed her brow with one hand. Then: God, I guess so, but more.

More what?

More, she sought around for the thing that was in her head that she'd never fitted words to. More like . . . when I have you, when I have you like that even, it's not enough and I still want some more of you. When you say something, I want to hear you say more and when you go someplace, any place, I want you to come back more than anything. That's pretty much been true for forever. That's what I mean.

He listened.

Well, she said, wearied, that's the whole truth. She checked the inside of her for any sign of falseness and it was not there. The glimpse she caught of herself this time in the passenger mirror was all eyes — red-rimmed, wide open.

Okay, he said and nodded and lifted his foot off the brake and dropped the truck into first so it swagged backward before the gear caught and he drove the rest of the way up the gravel drive. When he parked the truck, he did not look at her, but only shut the door behind him so that she was left alone in the cab. She waited on her side. She knew he was angry, but she waited all the same, because they had just married and a part of her hoped he might do something loving like carry her across the threshold of the house, which of course he did not, she knew it was foolish to even think it. When Orren reached the porch without once looking back, Aloma unlatched her own door with a sigh, let it fall heavily against its joints, bouncing and creaking into silence. By the time she followed onto the porch, Orren had already passed into the house. Aloma pulled the door gently shut behind her and stood holding the knob, leaning against it. Orren had pulled out a chair from the dining room table and sat down, taking his cigarettes out of his pocket and placing them before him on the table along with his keys and the change from his trousers. He pushed his chair back so that his legs splayed out from the seat. He looked across the table out the window. The edges of her mouth turned down, Aloma gazed helplessly around her at the house, which did not speak to her of a home and maybe never would. Its wall of untold faces, the buckling piano, the memories which were not her own. Her eyes settled on Orren.

Let's get rid of this piano, she said. It's done.

He squinted as though at something a long ways off out the window, something he could not quite see, but to her surprise, he said, Maybe so.

And maybe move some of these pictures. We don't need them all on one wall.

If you want, he said. Still, he would not look in her direction and so she crossed the room until she stood beside him, and frustrated, she said, Orren. But he sat, he just sat. So she hiked up her dress around her thighs and straddled her legs over his on the chair and unfolded his arms, which had been crossed over his chest, and placed his hands on her hips. Orren, she said and this time he looked at her because he could not do otherwise, but he did not resist when she kissed him and then he kissed her hard and when the chair nearly tipped, they lay on the floor, not bothering to remove their clothing because they did not have any time to spare, as all things both bad and good happen in an instant and they both knew it now, she and Orren both. And right after he came, before he could even catch his breath, while his face was still in the hair above her ear, his voice staggered in her ear, Don't let nobody in you but me.

Her eyes, closed and all submitted, flashed open at once. What, she snapped. We get married and that's the first thing you say to me?

He raised his head so his face was over hers. She saw the beads of sweat on his lip and the high ruddiness in his cheeks. I mean it, he said.

God, Orren, she said. Don't boss me and fuck me at the same time, and she slid out from under him and hunted around for her underwear until she found it and she struggled back into it under her dress, feeling wet and undone. Her legs shook a little. Orren just lay there on the floor and watched her, and when she stepped over him to leave the room, he tucked himself into his pants and sat up, slowly. He put his head in his hands.

She turned around at the doorway to the kitchen. The thing with you, Orren, is you never ever say the right thing, she said and made to leave, but stopped abruptly. Her words knocked about the height of the house and came back to her. She listened to them echoing for a moment. Then she said much slower, in a tone stripped of rancor, without turning this time, Orren, don't let's fight this day or ever again, and she meant it as she said it, though she heard how useless it was, all the longing and futility that it encompassed, and she saw too that she would say it again in her lifetime, perhaps many times, and that it would be as tiresome then as it was now. She found suddenly that she was fatigued — mostly with herself — and she sagged sideways against the doorjamb and might have fallen over had it not been there, unyielding. Behind her she could hear Orren breathing, silent again. Suddenly Aloma straightened up and passed through the kitchen and out the back, but once there, she did not know where to go, she only knew that it was trouble in the house and trouble out of the house and there was nothing she could do about it short of trying on a new self, and she did not know how to do that. She couldn't trust the world to make her happy for more than a minute at a time, and generally less than that, but her life had to be borne. She looked out toward the mountains and rolled her eyes. She had married someone who was fastened to this place, to these foothills, and she could not understand him no matter how hard she tried. She was no closer to that knowledge now that they were married than when they were not. And just as she was thinking these thoughts and sinking down in fatigue on the crumbling steps where she had fallen and scarred herself three months prior, just as she was thinking, Is it really him who makes me unhappy or is it just me after all, just then he appeared from behind her in the kitchen, a cigarette in his mouth.

Don't smoke in the house, Aloma said.

He nodded. His hair was rumpled. He stepped down onto the concrete step above her. He looked out at the mountains and his face eased up just barely, but enough so that even seated beneath him on the second step, she saw it. She turned to the mountains and looked out too, but she did not know what he saw. She only knew that it pleased him.

She rose then and she was gazing up into his face, which was still above her, and she was taking his hand and he let her guide him off the steps and down the hill away from the house. His hand was large in hers, which was as small as a child's except she was no child, she was leading him, their fingers dovetailed.

You want to see that hobber again, he said after they'd gone twenty paces in the direction of the stock barn.

No, she said. She did not lead him to the calf, though it was there by the gate waiting when they walked up, its young legs firm now under its wide baby belly. It turned its head when they approached.

Haddy, Orren said to the calf and it stepped back from the gate as if it knew they would come through and pass their hands along its soft early hide, which they did as they walked on. The gate swung shut behind them and they picked their way through the pasture. The calf juned along beside them for a few feet and bawled once so loud that it startled Aloma and she drew her shoulders up toward her ears and laughed. Still she held tight to Orren's hand and they walked past the barn where the chickens nested on the shadowed wall and a new red-and-black rooster tightroped the empty crib near the barn door. The few cows dotting the pasture followed them as they walked the worn cowtrace on the hill, they leaned forward and lost their breath a little on its upward slope. When they came to the treeline, Orren said, Where are you taking me? She only smiled and they walked into the cooler air of the woods and two cows followed them into the shade. Orren looked back at them and shook his head and looked at Aloma and shook his head again, but he followed on without comment. The cows came on unhurried legs. At the back fence, Aloma said, Up and over, and Orren went first and helped her over the barbed wire, bunching the hem of her dress in his hand so it wouldn't snag. The cows, having stopped a few feet back, watched them intently and then, as if agreeing together that they could not scale the fence, turned like two black ships and gaited slowly toward the sunlight in the field. Beyond the fence, Aloma walked, turning from side to side, trying to recall the exact shape of the tree, the black of the bark, and Orren watched her with one eyebrow raised and just as he was reaching into his pocket for his cigarettes, she said, Come here, Orren.

He walked over to where she stood and appraised the tree, saw the $E + C$, and his face did not alter. But his hand remained as still as a photograph over his breast pocket where he had been reaching when the letters penetrated his understanding. He blinked.

Now, how did I never . . . he said, very evenly, and then his hand shook as if it were deciding whether to take a cigarette or do something else altogether and then it reached up and covered his eyes and he stood there, not moving. A crow sounded in the trees above them as it passed, they heard the winnowing of its wings. Aloma stood beside him and traced a hand over the graven bark and the frets of the carving scraped against her fingertips. The flesh of the tree was hard now, it passed the impression of permanence. She waited patiently for Orren, looking into the half of his face that was not covered.

How long do you think it's been here? said Aloma.

Orren lowered his hand, blinked, and shook his head. I don't know. Thirty years. Maybe more. From when they first met maybe.

She looked past the tree toward where the house stood, hidden by the turning foliage, and he followed her gaze, then he patted his hand over his breast pocket a few times and exhaled. He looked up at the trees and she did too, at the way the sunlight penetrated the dense leaves to the spot where they stood, touching the bark of the carved tree, the ground underfoot, even their faces. Orren looked down at her. Then he took her hand and led her back out of the woods, across the pasture, and up to the old house.

We do hope that you have enjoyed reading this large print book.

Did you know that all of our titles are available for purchase?

We publish a wide range of high quality large print books including:
Romances, Mysteries, Classics
General Fiction
Non Fiction and Westerns

Special interest titles available in large print are:
The Little Oxford Dictionary
Music Book
Song Book
Hymn Book
Service Book

Also available from us courtesy of Oxford University Press:
Young Readers' Dictionary
(large print edition)
Young Readers' Thesaurus
(large print edition)

For further information or a free brochure, please contact us at:
Ulverscroft Large Print Books Ltd.,
The Green, Bradgate Road, Anstey,
Leicester, LE7 7FU, England.
Tel: (00 44) **0116 236 4325**
Fax: (00 44) **0116 234 0205**

Other titles published by
The House of Ulverscroft:

A GIRL MADE OF DUST

Nathalie Abi-Ezzi

1980s Lebanon. Eight-year-old Ruba lives in a village outside Beirut. From her family home she can see the city's buildings and hear the rumble of shelling. As civil war tears the country apart, Ruba has her own worries — while her mother toils and struggles for money, her father avoids work and family. When Ruba decides that she must save him, she uncovers a secret which sets her on a journey from childhood to the beginnings of adulthood. But Israeli troops invade Lebanon; danger comes ever closer, and Ruba realises that she may not be able to keep her family safe.